THEIR BORDER L

Men of the Border Lands 5

Marla Monroe

MENAGE EVERLASTING

Siren Publishing, Inc.
www.SirenPublishing.com

A SIREN PUBLISHING BOOK
IMPRINT: Ménage Everlasting

THEIR BORDER LANDS GIFT
Copyright © 2012 by Marla Monroe

ISBN: 978-1-62241-168-9

First Printing: July 2012

Cover design by Les Byerley
All art and logo copyright © 2012 by Siren Publishing, Inc.

Printed in the U.S.A.

PUBLISHER
Siren Publishing, Inc.
www.SirenPublishing.com

THEIR BORDER LANDS GIFT

Men of the Border Lands 5

MARLA MONROE
Copyright © 2012

Chapter One

"Don't do this to me. Please, Mike. You can take care of me just fine."

"Kate, it's for your safety. I'll do whatever it takes to make sure you'll be safe and happy." Mike closed the suitcase and zipped it.

"I won't be happy if you pawn me off on some stranger. How could you do that?" she demanded.

"I'm not going to pawn you off to a stranger. I'm going to check them out and be sure they're good men first."

"Men! Are you serious? More than one man? Not no, but hell no! I'm not living with two men. Get that out of your head right now." Kate had been pacing back and forth, but stopped to plant her hands on her hips.

"Kate, I can't take care of you alone. You need two men. That way someone will always be close to you when the other is working. You've nearly been stolen four times now. I'd never forgive myself if you ended up with some wife beater, or worse, in a brothel. Mom would roll over in her grave if I let that happen to you."

Kate hung her head and let the silent tears slip out. She refused to show fear. She would be angry and worried, but never show fear. But fear of the unknown threatened to overwhelm her. How could he do this to her, his own sister?

Ever since the year of catastrophes when tornadoes, hurricanes, tsunamis, earthquakes and then disease had all but destroyed mankind, women had been scarce so that men fought over them. They stole them, sold them, and used them like slaves. So far, Kate had managed to stay safe with her brother looking after her. He didn't think their luck would hold out and had decided to take her to the Border Lands where there were fewer people.

He hoped to find not one, but two men he trusted to take her. Well, she was having none of it. She would figure something out before she let them use her.

Kate had been nineteen when everything went to hell. Now six years later, at twenty-five, she resented that her younger brother by two years had so much control over her. Sighing, she acknowledged that he had taken good care of her and kept her safe all this time. Still, she thought he was wrong in believing that finding two good men to take care of her was the right thing to do. She felt like he was just looking for someone to take her off his hands.

"Kate, you know I love you. I just want you to be happy, and right now, we're both running scared." Mike hugged her.

"I'm not scared. Maybe you are, but I'm not. I can take care of myself if you don't want to be burdened with me anymore. I expect you want to find your own woman. I can understand that, but looking for two men? Really, Mike. That's over the top."

"Damn it, Kate. I'm telling you it's for the best."

Kate noticed he didn't deny wanting a woman of his own. She sighed and tried to reason with him.

"Best for them, maybe, but certainly not for me. I don't want two men bossing me around, telling me what to do."

"I won't let you go to just anyone, Kate. I'll make sure they are good men who will treasure you and take care of you first. Do you think so little of me?" He frowned, looking hurt.

"Mike. I know you think you are doing the right thing, but you're not thinking it through. Once one man has control over a woman in today's world, he takes advantage of her. You've seen it. What do you really think it would be like with two men?"

"I promise. I won't let anyone hurt you. I'm going to make sure they are caring men," Mike said.

"And just how do you expect to do that? Anyone can pretend for as long as it takes to convince you."

Mike closed his eyes and let out a long breath. He just shook his head and turned away to carry the suitcase to the truck and travel trailer.

Kate followed him and watched him add her suitcase to the stack of provisions. She prayed they wouldn't end up in a wasteland somewhere without food or water. He claimed to have a map to the Border Lands and Barter Town. Where he had gotten it, she had no idea. He had been talking to someone about all of this for a long time evidently, because he had it all planned out.

"Hand me that box next to your foot, Kate." He reached down as she handed it up to him.

"I can't believe I'm helping you take me to my nightmare," she fumed under her breath.

"What was that?" Mike asked as he settled the box between two other boxes.

"Nothing."

He frowned at her with eyebrows that almost touched. He acted exasperated with her. Well, she was totally aggravated with him. She had to think of something before they reached the Border Lands. If not, she was lost.

Two hours later, Mike pronounced them packed and ready to leave at first light in the morning.

"We'll get up at four and be on the road by five, or a little after. I want to make the most of the light."

"Does that map tell you how long we'll be on the road?" she asked sarcastically.

"I figure it will take us a good four, maybe five days to reach Barter Town. You have to stick close to me there. That's a prime place for being kidnapped."

"Then why take me there at all?" She didn't understand his thinking on the subject.

"Because by then we'll need supplies, gas, and directions to the communities around there. Believe me. I wouldn't take you to that place for anything if I had a choice."

Kate pressed her lips together to keep from saying something she would ultimately regret.

* * * *

Early the next morning, Kate climbed up into the truck and settled in for the long drive ahead of them. Mike was busy checking the back of the truck and the camper they were pulling. They would sleep in it at night. She supposed she should be grateful for that. She'd heard that many people had to find places to sleep on the way out there.

Her brother climbed into the truck and smiled at her before starting it up and pulling out of the circular drive. She turned around to watch the only house she had ever lived in disappear from sight. One of the lucky few families, they hadn't lost their house in any of the catastrophes. They'd sustained a little damage here and there, but it had survived where her parents hadn't. They'd died in the plagues that ravaged the nation soon after everything else.

She knew she was saying good-bye to a way of life. Nothing would ever be the same.

"Are you going to leave me and go somewhere else? You're all I've got, Mike."

"I'll settle down somewhere close enough that we can see each other. I wouldn't leave you totally on your own." He turned and smiled at her, grabbing her hand in the process.

He squeezed it then returned his to the steering wheel.

"Then why can't we settle somewhere together? Then if I find someone I like…"

"Kate, we've been over this. Two can keep you safer than one. It's too dangerous now for you to be by yourself while I'm out working. End of discussion." His knuckles turned white where he was gripping the steering wheel.

She gritted her teeth and turned to stare out the side window at the passing scenery without really seeing it. All she could think about was that he was throwing her away. She loved him more than anything, but right then, she could have strangled him.

They reached a small town near lunchtime and pulled into a gas station. A young man of about twenty-four or so walked out of the building and up to the window on Mike's side.

"What can I do for you?" he asked with a huge smile on his face.

"We need to fill up. Do you take credits, or do you want to barter?"

"We take credits if you have them."

They negotiated a price, and the man turned away to fill the tank.

When he came back for his credits a little while later, Mike asked him if there was a place to eat that took credits.

"Just Janie's house. She cooks out of it and will fix you something if you ask," the young man told him.

"Thanks." Mike rolled up his window and cranked the truck.

They pulled out of the station and back onto the road. Mike followed the directions to Janie's house and pulled up outside a large house in desperate need of painting. It looked in good repair other than that. Kate hoped the food was edible.

Less than two hours later, they had finished eating and were back on the highway heading to the west. Heavy clouds filled the sky promising rain in the not too distant future. She dreaded the rain since it made driving dangerous with the truck pulling the trailer. Mike would be nervous the entire time.

She sighed when the first fat drops began to hit the windshield with echoing *splat* sounds. She hesitated at asking Mike to pull over since she was sure he would take offense. Still, as the rain grew heavier and the road more difficult to see, she bit the bullet and spoke.

"Maybe we should take a breather while it's raining so hard, Mike."

"I was just thinking the same thing. I wish I had pulled over earlier so we could have gotten in the back and rested." He pulled off the road at the first opportunity where there was enough blacktop to support them. Not that there was any other traffic that they had seen on the road, but they didn't want to be in the way if there was.

"How much longer till we stop for the night?" she asked.

"I figure if the rain stops fairly soon, we'll drive until we reach the next town and stay there for the night." Mike rubbed a hand over the windshield to clear the fog so he could see.

They remained stuck on the side of the road for nearly an hour before the rain passed them by. Finally, the clouds parted and the sun poked a few rays through to signal the end. Mike pulled back on the highway and continued toward the next little spot on the map.

* * * *

They pulled out early the next morning after a meager breakfast of peanut butter and crackers. Mike wanted to ration out their supplies until he knew how far they were actually driving. It was nearly one in the afternoon by the time they pulled into a little truck stop that looked occupied. They were low on fuel, and Mike said he didn't want to chance running out by pushing on to the next town.

"Stay in the truck, and keep the doors locked no matter what." Mike climbed out of the truck and hit the door lock before closing the door.

Kate bit her lower lip as she watched her brother walk across the parking lot then disappear inside the building. She waited for what seemed like forever without any sign of Mike. Just when she had decided to go inside to look for him, he pushed through the door of the station and walked back toward her. She watched his face closely for any sign of what he was thinking.

He reached the truck and started getting ready to pump the gas. She blew out a breath in relief. He didn't look happy, but he was pumping the gas and seemed to be okay. She waited until he walked around to the driver's door to unlock the truck.

"What's wrong?" she demanded as soon as he climbed in.

"They basically cleaned me out of credits. They kept saying that there wasn't anything between here and Gateway. What do you want to bet there are half a freaking dozen when we head that way?" Mike started the truck and pulled out of the truck stop a little faster than was necessary.

Sure enough, they passed two more gas stations on the way to Gateway. They pulled into Gateway around seven that night and gassed up at a little station on the edge of town. A man walked out and smiled at them. He looked to be in his middle thirties and was beefy.

"What can I do for you?"

"We want to barter for some gas. What do you need?"

"Don't rightly need much of anything, but if you have something for my wife, I'd appreciate it. Something girly." He leered at Kate. "I bet you've got something pretty for my wife, don't you, honey?"

"Kate?" Mike took her hand. "Do you have anything like that? I'll get it for you."

"What color eyes does she have?" Kate asked, trying to think of what she had with her.

"Sue Ann! Come on out here, woman, and meet these nice people." The man yelled back over his shoulder toward the building.

A small, waifish woman who couldn't have been much older than twenty-one eased out of the station and walked toward the man. A bruise covered the left side of her face and eye. Immediately Kate wanted to take her with them, but knew that would never happen.

"Get my training case out of the back, and I'll find something nice for her."

"Keep your doors locked until I get back. Don't roll down your window either." Mike climbed out of the truck and locked the door behind him.

"Where you heading, pretty lady?" the man asked, squeezing the woman close to him.

"We've got relatives out west, and we're going to move there with them."

Mike walked up to the truck, and she reached over and unlocked the door so he could climb in with her case. She opened it and rummaged around until she found what she was looking for. She handed Mike a tube of lipstick and a pretty silver barrette that would look good in the woman's brown hair.

Mike climbed back out of the truck, locking the door, and walked around to give the man the items. The man took them and handed them over to the woman. She smiled wide as the sky and teared up. She looked up at Kate and mouthed *thank you*. Kate smiled back at her and waved her hand. The man shooed the woman back into the station and proceeded to pump their gas.

Her brother got back into the truck and waited for the man to finish filling the truck up. Once that was done, he waved them off. Mike pulled out of the station and headed into the sleepy little town of Gateway. He refused to look at her. No doubt he knew what she was thinking.

"Don't say it," Mike interrupted her when she would have pointed out that it could have been her.

"Don't you see, Mike? You never know if someone will be kind or mean. How can you chance it with me?"

"Fuck it, Kate! I'm doing the best I can for you." Mike wasn't known for cursing, so she knew she had upset him. *Good.*

She crossed her arms and turned away from him. There was no reasoning with him like he was now. He'd argue with a fence post. Kate swallowed down the tears threatening to fall only to find a giant lump in her throat. She couldn't understand why he thought he could choose someone safe without knowing them. He was desperate. That was the bottom line. Mike was scared he would screw up, and she would get taken while he was supposed to be watching her.

She leaned her head against the hot window and stared ahead at the dilapidated houses on either side of the street. No doubt there were other desperate people living in them, wondering where their next meal would be coming from or if they would wake up the next day.

They spent the night on the other side of the little town after negotiating some food for some clothes. Evidently most of the stores were out of the necessities, and the supply trucks were never predictable.

"We'll reach Barter Town the day after tomorrow around lunchtime. I want you to remember to keep close to me, and if anyone asks, we're husband and wife. We don't exactly look that much alike with your honey-colored hair and mine being a lighter blond instead of your richer gold." Mike checked the tires on the trailer as he talked when they were getting ready to leave the next morning.

"I know. Don't worry. I'll stick to you like glue. I have no wish to be stolen and sold to someone," she said sarcastically.

"I'm not selling you, Kate!"

"Oh, no. I'm not worth anything. You're giving me away."

"Damn it." He stomped off to the front of the truck and climbed in the cab.

He started the truck, but waited for her to walk around and get in as well. Neither of them talked much the rest of the day or when they stopped for the night. She knew better than to wander off, but kept her distance from him until they went to bed that night.

Kate tossed and turned, dreaming of strange men pawing at her and kissing her. She woke up tired the next morning, with a serious headache. She took the painkillers they had and prayed it would help. Today they would reach Barter Town, and she didn't want to be sick when she needed to be at her best and aware of everything around her.

Chapter Two

When they reached Barter Town, Kate could tell that Mike was even more nervous than before. They bartered for some gas, and after the way the men everywhere tried to get a look at Kate, he decided that it was too dangerous for her to go with him to barter for more food and water.

"It's worse than what they said, Kate. I can't hold you and barter for what we need at the same time. Someone will snatch you from me for sure. You're going to have to stay in the trailer until I get back," he said.

"How long will you be?" Kate wasn't getting a good feeling about this at all.

"Not long, I hope. It will be hot back there since it's just a little past noon, but the water is back there. You can drink plenty while you wait."

"I wish we didn't have to stop here at all," Kate muttered.

Mike pulled the truck into a parking place under a tree for shade and got out to help her in the back. He closed and locked the door once she was inside. He slapped the door once and was gone.

Kate huddled in the back of the camper, waiting on Mike to return for what seemed like hours. Surely he wouldn't look for someone here to take her. Not in this godforsaken spot. Someone fiddled with the door to the camper. Since Mike had the key, Kate knew it couldn't be him. When the door suddenly wrenched open, Kate couldn't stop the tiny scream from escaping.

"Well, what do we have here?" a man's voice asked.

Kate slipped down beneath the table and curled up into a ball under it.

The man climbed up in the camper and approached her. She couldn't see him in the dim light with the bright sunlight glaring from behind him. His face was in shadow.

"Think I found me a little woman to play with." He walked further into the camper and knelt down to look under the table.

Of course he knew where she was. He would have had a bird's-eye view of her from the doorway before he climbed up.

"Come out, girlie. I can see you back there. I won't hurt you."

"My br—husband will be back in a few minutes, and you'll be sorry you broke into our trailer."

"Aw, well, we'll be long gone by then. Come on out before you make me mad," he said.

"No!" She tried to push even tighter underneath the table, but the wall was uncooperative in letting her go further.

He reached in, and she slapped at his hand. When he tried to grab her hair, she bit his hand.

"Bitch! You'll be sorry you did that."

He climbed under the table and grabbed her hair with two hands before she had a chance to bite him again. He yanked and pulled until she was following him out of sheer pain.

When she attempted to run, he grabbed her around the waist and stopped her. She screamed, but no one came to help as he dragged her out of the camper and out onto the street. She kicked back and tried to butt him with her head into his chin, but he managed to avoid her pitiful attempts at breaking free.

"Let go of me. Someone help me! He's kidnapping me," she screamed. Still, no one paid any real attention other than a passing interest. Kate tried scratching at his hands with her nails, but he retaliated by squeezing her until she couldn't breathe. Tears flowed from her eyes as he started to carry her away.

"Let her go," another man's voice said.

"She's mine, so butt out of what ain't your business," her captor said.

Kate looked up into the darkest eyes she had ever seen. His long black hair was pulled back into a ponytail, and he looked ready to do bodily harm. Standing next to him was another man with shoulder-length, shaggy brown hair and hazel eyes that seemed to be trying to tell her something.

"She says she's not," the brown-haired man said.

"They all say that. You know that," her captor said.

"I'm not his. My husband is out bartering for supplies. This man broke into our camper. You can look at the door and see where he did."

Her captor slapped a hand hard against her face, covering her mouth. She would have a bruise there for sure. She tried head-butting him again, but his hand over her mouth prevented her from any real movement. Kate began to feel as if she were suffocating despite being able to breathe through her nose. His smell made her nauseous so that she didn't want to do it.

"There you go. She already has a husband. Put her down before we have to do something about it." This came from the dark-haired man. He had a voice so deep it stirred something low in her belly.

Kate continued to struggle though it did little good. The two men advanced on them. Her captor couldn't run with her, so he threatened to break her neck and wrapped an arm around it against her chin.

"I'll snap her neck so fast you won't have a chance of getting to her."

"Kate! What's going on here! That's my wife. Let go of her now."

Kate closed her eyes in relief to hear Mike's voice. Surely he could talk some sense into the man.

"I don't see no ring on her finger. As I see it, she's free for the taking," the man said.

"Let her go, now, before you make us angry," the dark-haired stranger said in a low voice.

Mike advanced on the man. He swung Kate around to face Mike, nearly doing as he said he would and breaking her neck. She began to have trouble breathing as his grip was cutting off her air supply.

So preoccupied with trying to breathe, she missed it when the other two men grabbed her captor from behind and jerked her from his grip. She heard a bone break. She was so afraid it was her neck that she began to struggle just to know that she still could.

From somewhere, she heard a scream, but knew it wasn't hers. Strong but gentle arms pulled her back against a firm chest. Then there were soothing words in her ear.

"Easy, Kate. I've got you. Nothing is going to happen to you. Your husband is right here. Everything's going to be all right now."

"Give her to me." Mike's voice didn't even soothe her as much as the stranger's voice had.

She was carefully passed off to Mike, who hugged her and kissed the top of her head.

"Thank you for helping us." Mike stuck out his hand to shake. "I'm Mike and this is my—wife, Kate Shaw."

"Pleased to meet you, and glad we could be of help. I'm Bruce Hannover, and this is my brother, Marcus."

They shook hands, and Kate couldn't help but stare at them. They were good-looking men with broad shoulders and wide chests that tapered down to small waists. Their muscular arms promised that they would have muscles all over. She'd felt Marcus's muscles against her back.

"Where are you headed?" Bruce asked.

"Looking to settle around these parts. Just haven't gotten that far. I had to stop and get gas and supplies. I never dreamed anyone would actually break into my camper." Mike shook his head, still holding Kate close to him.

"You can't trust anyone around here. There's no real law here." Marcus crossed his arms.

"Is that why you're not worried that you broke that man's arm?" Mike asked.

"That, and I don't care. He deserved it. Your woman is going to have bruises on her. He deserved a lot worse," Bruce told him.

"We really are grateful to you. Do you have your own woman?"

The two men sighed. Bruce walked off with his hands on his hips.

Marcus looked out after him. "We did. She was killed by a wolf while we were out working in the pasture." His jaw muscles worked as if he were trying to keep from showing his bitterness.

"I'm sorry." Kate didn't know where her voice came from after being so terrified.

"Thanks. Bruce blames himself. He doesn't talk about her."

"I'm so sorry I brought it up," Mike said.

"No. It's okay. He needs to come to grips with it and get over it. We never thought a wolf would come up in the yard like that. They never had before."

"Well, we need to get going. I thank you both again."

Mike walked her around to the passenger side of the truck and helped her in the cab before locking the door and closing it. Then he loaded up the supplies in the back of the truck and secured the camper door the best he could. He nodded to the two men then climbed up into the truck and started the engine. They pulled out of the parking lot and headed toward the open road.

"Where are we going?" Kate finally asked.

"I picked a spot on the map that looks like there should be plenty of houses. We'll pick an empty one and set up in it."

"See why I don't want you to just give me to someone? You don't have any idea who will be nice and who won't. I doubt there are any nice men left out this direction." Kate looked over at where her brother was gripping the steering wheel with both hands.

"What about those two men who helped us?"

"Well, they're obviously still grieving for their wife. I think we'll be hard pressed to find anyone else that nice in this godforsaken land."

"Don't you get it, Kate? If it had been just me, I would have lost you to that bastard. I couldn't have taken him. He was nearly twice as big as me. It took those two men to get you away from him." He slapped the steering wheel with the palm of his hand.

"I'm okay, Mike. He didn't get me."

"He hurt you, Kate, and I couldn't do a damn thing about it."

"I'm sorry, Mike. I know I'm making things hard for you. I wish I could take care of myself."

"Oh, hell. Don't go blaming yourself. It's not your fault the world's gone to hell. You shouldn't have to be able to defend yourself. You shouldn't have to hide in the back of the damn camper while I go bartering for supplies so we can live. This whole thing is fucked up."

Kate didn't say anything. She knew he was frustrated, but must of all, he was scared, and she wouldn't call him on that.

* * * *

Bruce climbed up into the cab of their truck then waited on Marcus to do the same before pulling out of Barter Town and heading toward home.

"I liked her. She didn't get hysterical when her husband came up." Marcus looked over at Bruce.

"*Husband* being the operative word, Marcus." Bruce stared straight ahead.

"Yeah, but she was pretty and feisty. It doesn't hurt to look."

"She's another man's wife, for God's sakes," Bruce all but yelled.

"Hey, calm down, Bruce. What's gotten into you?"

"Sorry. I'm just keyed up over the fight and thinking about what could have happened to that poor woman if we hadn't walked up when we did. Her husband needs to keep her away from Barter Town. He can't possibly keep her safe alone."

"Yeah, you're right about that. I'm guessing he's figured that out, though." Marcus sighed.

Bruce felt guilty because he had fussed at Marcus for something he was even now doing, thinking about the pretty, honey-haired beauty. She was nothing like Irene. She'd had long blonde hair more white than the other woman's gold, and a tiny body that he had often worried he would crush beneath him. She had never complained and was always ready for their loving.

Still, he couldn't get Kate out of his mind. She had womanly curves and was probably around five feet five inches to his six foot three. He wouldn't crush her beneath him while loving her. He and Marcus had never taken Irene together because of her small build, but he had no doubt they could take Kate together. Then he realized he was lusting after another man's wife and hit the steering wheel in frustration.

Marcus, for once, wisely remained quiet.

They arrived at their home deep within the Border Lands at the farthest possible location they could drive without gassing up. When they had lost Irene, he'd insisted they move so they wouldn't be reminded of her everywhere they turned. Their new home was too big for just them, but it had prime grazing land for their cattle and a garden spot already cut, though overgrown. It hadn't taken much work to turn it into a rich garden.

They climbed out of the truck and began unloading in silence. They tended to do most everything in silence now, where before they laughed and talked and teased one another. Despite it having been nearly two years now since they'd buried her, they still hadn't buried her memory.

It was nearly dark by the time they had everything unloaded and put away. They fixed a dinner of soup and sandwiches then sat in the living room where they discussed what they would work on the next day. When the conversation lagged, Bruce began to think about Kate and how her rounded ass was perfect for fucking. He'd come to the conclusion they had been too long without a woman and should have looked for one to share while they had been in town. He loathed using the brothel there, but surely they could treat a woman well and make her day a little brighter having been with them. He shook his head. No, he couldn't see supporting their abuse of the women.

"What are you shaking your head about over there?" Marcus asked.

"Just thinking that maybe I could use a good fucking to clear my mind. It's been a long time since we shared a woman."

"I'm not going to that brothel in Barter Town," Marcus immediately said.

"That's what I was shaking my head about. Neither am I. So, we're stuck using our hands and dreaming about someone who's long dead. What a fucking laugh."

"Bruce, it wasn't your fault."

"One of us should have always been with her. I should have gone hunting that wolf the first time we saw the tracks out in the woods." Bruce rubbed his face with both hands.

"We'd never seen the wolf. How were we to know it would attack a human? They don't unless you threaten them." Marcus leaned forward with his elbows resting on his knees.

"I'm over here thinking about fucking another man's wife after I fussed at you earlier. I can't get her out of my mind, and that's wrong, Marcus."

"It's natural when she's the first woman we've seen that wasn't wearing a damn collar and chain. Besides, she was pretty and brave. That's a heady combination in a woman to us."

Bruce closed his eyes and tried to picture Irene's delicate features, but they kept getting mixed up with Kate's warm, amber-brown eyes and kissable lips. He felt guilty for a few seconds then decided it had been long enough that he shouldn't. He had mourned her for nearly two years now. It was time to move on when he was attracted to another woman, especially another man's wife.

"It's time we went to bed. Dawn comes early, and we have a lot to do since we were gone all day today." Bruce stood up and stretched.

They turned down the oil lamps, taking one apiece to their respective rooms. Bruce used the master bathroom though he slept in one of the spare rooms, as did Marcus. Marcus used the hall bathroom.

Bruce turned on the water to the shower and adjusted it to suit his tastes. Then he pulled out a towel and bath cloth while trying to imagine something besides Kate's desperate face.

Chapter Three

Mike drove them deep into the mountainous area until he found a house that looked empty. They got out and explored only to find that the roof was gone from the back half. Once again they climbed in the truck and followed the road until they came to another drive. This one looked well used, so they skipped it and continued driving.

"It's getting dark, Mike. What are we going to do?" Kate didn't like the idea of being lost in the mountains at night.

"We're going to check one last address then turn around and find a place to park and sleep for the night."

"Maybe we should try another road. This one looks like it goes all the way to Canada to me. We'll run out of gas before we can get back to get more."

"I've got it figured out, Kate. We have twenty-five more miles before we have to turn around, and I have five gallons of gas stored if we need it in case I miscalculated. I've got it under control, Kate."

"Okay, okay. You know I don't like driving in the dark and especially not on unfamiliar roads." Kate had a death grip on her seatbelt.

"Look, help me watch for the next drive. It should be close now." The map where he'd marked all the houses had come from the courthouse. He'd bought it from one of the men in Barter Town. "We're almost at the end of the line I drew."

Several minutes later, Kate pointed out an overgrown drive on the left.

"Is that it?" she asked.

"Looks like it. Hold on. It's going to be a bumpy ride."

They followed the drive for nearly a mile before it dead-ended at a small house that looked in fair shape. It had all of its windows and doors from what Kate could see, but they would need to look at it all over to know for sure what sort of shape it was in.

"It's getting dark fast, Mike. Maybe we should wait until tomorrow to check it out."

"I think you're probably right. Let's sleep in the camper then get up early and see if it will be livable or not."

They climbed out of the cab of the truck and walked through the tall grass to the trailer. Mike unhooked the broken lock and helped her climb up in back. She grabbed one of the flashlights and started fixing their beds. She was hungry, but they'd eaten their meal several hours earlier. She didn't feel like trying to come up with something to eat now.

"Climb on up on the bed, Kate. I'll close everything down and bed down on the floor." Mike secured the camper door with some wire and a small board he'd picked up from somewhere. Then he settled down on the makeshift bed on the floor.

"I think this one is going to be the one, Kate. Just wait and see."

"I hope you're right, Mike. I'm tired of riding. I just want to set up housekeeping and let that be that." She hoped he would forget about trying to find her a couple of husbands if they were far enough out that no one would bother them.

If he found a woman he wanted to settle down with, they could live there as well. What was wrong with that? Families all lived together nowadays like they used to in the past. She'd give them all the privacy they could want. She just didn't want to end up belonging to two overbearing brutes who would order her around.

"I can hear you thinking clear down here. What is it, Kate?" Mike's voice startled her out of her thoughts.

"Nothing. I'm just wondering how we're going to plant a garden if we don't have a plow to plow it."

"You let me worry about that part. You'll have enough to worry over in the house."

Kate rolled her eyes, but wisely kept her mouth shut. Mike took his role as head of the house very seriously. She sighed. Obviously, since he was dead set on finding her a husband or two.

Kate grew sleepy and finally let her exhaustion claim her.

* * * *

"Wake up, Kate."

Mike shook her shoulder again. She wanted to slap his hand away, but knew they needed to get up and get on the road again. Then she remembered that they had found a house to look at and were in the front yard camping out.

She opened one eye and groaned at the light pouring in from the side window where he'd opened the curtains.

"What time is it?" she asked.

"It's just after seven. We need to see about the house so we can move on if it's not livable."

Kate rolled out of the little bed and stepped over his makeshift bed that he hadn't bothered to pick up. She rolled everything up and replaced the covers at the foot of her bed. Then she pulled out the last of the peanut butter and stale crackers. They quickly ate, washing it down with bottled water.

"You ready?" Mike asked. He acted like a kid at Christmas.

"I guess so. Let's take the flashlights with us." She picked up one while Mike grabbed the other.

He helped her down from the camper, and they slowly made their way around the outside of the house to look at the back. Everything looked intact. There was even what looked like a shed with a tractor in it. *If only it would work.*

They climbed up on the back porch, which seemed to be sturdy and in good repair. Mike tried the door and found the screen unlocked. He tried the door itself, but it was locked. He went from window to window until he found one open on the side of the house.

"You stay right by the window until I come back and tell you it's safe to climb in."

"I'm not going anywhere." She sighed and watched as her brother climbed through the window into the house. She could hear him moving around inside but lost sight of him when he turned a corner.

"You okay in there, Mike?" she called through the window.

"Yeah, I'll be right out to get you. Go around to the back door again. I'll let you in."

She sighed and walked around to the back of the house and climbed back up on the porch. Mike appeared in the window of the back door with a big grin on his face. He unlatched the back door and opened it for her to walk inside.

"Everything looks in good shape, Kate. I think we have a keeper." He was like a kid in a candy store showing her around.

"The water works! There's gas, but no electricity. I guess that was more than we could hope for."

"You're kidding. We have gas? I wonder how?" Kate hurried over to the stove and turned on the burner. It hissed but didn't light. She quickly turned it back off.

"We'll need to light the pilot light. I wonder if we have gas or electric hot water heaters. I could really use a hot bath."

"If we don't have gas, I can carry water from the stove so you can have a hot bath, Kate. You'll feel better in no time."

"I think what we need to do first is pick a room to clean and start cleaning."

"I'm going to have to leave that to you and start work on that old tractor out there. We've got to put a garden in before it's too late in the year." Mike hurried out the door, leaving Kate alone in the kitchen.

After all, I am the woman. It's my job to take care of the house. She sighed and decided the kitchen would be the first room to clean.

They could sleep in the camper another night or two if they needed to. She pulled everything out of the cabinets and stacked it on one end of the kitchen and got to work cleaning the room from top to bottom.

At some point, she heard the tractor start up. She walked over to the back door and looked through the screen to see Mike waving triumphantly as he drove the thing around the backyard. She waved back and went back to cleaning and putting the dishes away. By the time Mike returned to the house at dusk, she had the kitchen in working order and had started on one of the bathrooms.

"So, how did it go plowing?" she asked as he stripped off his boots.

"Got the old garden back there broken up, but it's going to take a lot of plowing to get it in planting shape. I'm not sure how much diesel is in the old tank back there, either."

"It will work out. I'm going to warm us up some soup for dinner tonight. How does that sound to you?"

"Good, but can you add something to it? I'm starved, and neither of us got lunch today."

"I'll fix it up with something. You need a bath. I've cleaned the majority of the bathroom. Go get cleaned up. You can handle a little cool water."

They made a meal out of canned soup and pinto beans. Then Mike carried hot water from the stove to the bathroom so that Kate could have a hot bath. She carried her clean clothes inside to change into when she dried off.

She sighed as soon as she slipped into the warm water. It wasn't exactly hot, but it was close. She hadn't had a real bath in a week. This was heaven as far as she was concerned. She quickly bathed then just relaxed against the back of the tub and let the warm water sink into her weary muscles.

"Kate! You okay in there?" Mike knocked on the door.

She huffed out a breath in annoyance. "I'm fine, Mike. I'm just enjoying having a bath."

"Well don't drown while I'm out moving our stuff inside."

Before she could stop him he was gone. *Great!* He would have them sleeping on something dirty if she didn't get out of the tub now and direct where to put their things. *Typical man.*

Kate climbed out of the tub and quickly dried off. She pulled on her clean clothes and raced out of the house to stop him.

"Don't, Mike."

"Don't what?" he asked, standing outside of the camper with his arms full.

"Nothing else is clean in the house yet. We're going to have to sleep in the camper another night so I can clean our bedrooms next."

"Oh. Didn't think about needing to clean them." He looked sheepish and tossed the stuff back in the camper.

Kate cringed at the mess he just made, but didn't say anything. It looked like most of it was his stuff anyway. She retraced her steps back into the house and cleaned up the bathroom from her bath. She looked at the tub longingly, but reminded herself she could have another bath tomorrow.

They sat up and talked about what they would work on next and how long it might take to finish everything that needed doing around the little house. Kate was feeling pretty good about the house and making it into a home until Mike brought up the subject of finding her a couple of husbands.

"I figure there are some decent men around here in this area working their land. In a few months, we can maybe meet some of them."

"How do you plan to do that?" She couldn't keep the sarcasm out of her voice.

"Kate," he began.

"No, we have a nice place here that between the two of us we can turn into a home. You can find yourself a woman and bring her home. I'll stay out of your way. Just don't send me off to live with a couple of strangers, Mike."

Mike got up and stomped off toward the camper. "I'm not going to discuss this with you again."

Kate pressed her lips together to keep from screaming at him. She sat on the porch long enough to let him get settled then made her way to the camper and climbed inside. He'd already lain down on the floor. She had to climb over him to get to the bed.

"Kate. I'm sorry. I just don't see that I have a choice. I can't keep you safe. There are black market thieves everywhere. If I'm out in the field plowing or out hunting for food, you're all alone here with no one to keep you safe. They could snatch you, and I'd never see you again."

"Let's just see how things go, Mike. Please?" She knew he would hear the tears in her voice. They rolled down her cheeks as she lay on the little bed.

He was silent for a long time then he sighed. "Okay, Kate. We'll see how things go."

Chapter Four

The weeks flew by as Kate turned the little three-bedroom house into a home for them. She helped Mike plant once he had the garden tilled within an inch of its life. They figured they had enough for the two of them for the winter. Kate studied the books they'd brought with them on canning and made a list of supplies they would need come harvest time.

"There's a city out this direction called Middleton where they say you can scavenge supplies. We probably need to make a run there and load up on whatever we can find," Mike told her one day.

"How far is it, Mike?" She wasn't really excited about leaving their home.

"About two hours' drive according to the map."

"Are you sure we need to go?"

Mike didn't seem to catch on that she wasn't happy about the planned trip.

"Yeah, we need to go and get whatever we can before there's nothing left. Plus, we need some things like those canning supplies you have on your list there." He pointed at her supply list. She almost covered it up.

"I don't like the idea of leaving the house, Mike. What if someone comes and steals stuff from us? Maybe I should stay and guard it while you go. I can shoot the gun as well as you can."

"Absolutely not. You go with me. I'm not leaving you here alone."

"Mike."

"No! End of discussion. We'll leave first thing in the morning. I'm going to clean out the truck and the camper. We'll need all the room we can squeeze out of them." Mike turned and walked out of the house leaving Kate to fume.

Early the next morning, they pulled down the drive and were about to pull out onto the road when Mike stopped for another truck coming down the road. It passed them but stopped a little piece down the road.

"Mike?"

"Shh, Kate. They're probably just interested in who their neighbors are."

The two men climbed out of the truck and walked back toward them. To everyone's surprise, it was the two men who'd helped save Kate back in Barter Town.

"Hi. Looks like we're neighbors," Mike said as they approached.

Both men walked over to Mike's side of the truck.

"You working the Crowley place? It was in pretty bad shape last time we saw it," Bruce said.

"We've been working on it for the last few weeks. Got a garden planted, so we'll be good for winter."

"Where you headed now?" Marcus asked with a smile.

"Middleton. I heard there are still some good pickings there, and we need supplies."

"That's where we are headed. You can follow us," Marcus told them.

"That's real nice of you. Thanks."

"Ma'am," Bruce said with a nod before walking back to their truck.

"They're good men," Mike said. "Too bad they're still mourning their poor wife."

"Mike!"

"Kate, I'm just making a statement. I'm not going to push you on them. That would be insensitive."

"For them or me?" she asked with a growl.

They rode in silence the entire drive to Middleton. Kate had a lot on her mind, including the two hunky men in the truck ahead of them. They were both strong men with kind eyes. She realized that she was attracted to them, and before she knew it, her panties were wet thinking about more than just saying hi.

She let herself imagine a scenario where they were her husbands and they worshiped the ground she walked on. To have the love of such men would be heaven, she decided.

"Kate. Are you listening to me?"

"No, sorry, what did you say?"

"I was saying that you need to keep close to me once we get there. They say the wolves are bad around the abandoned buildings. They make dens out of them."

"Great. Something else to worry about," she muttered.

They pulled into Middleton behind the other truck. It pulled off the side of the road just inside of town, and Bruce rolled down his window.

"If you follow this road straight through town, you'll hit all the major stores. Watch out for wolves. We're headed to the industrial park side for some parts we need," Bruce said.

"Thanks for letting us follow you in," Mike told them.

"Don't stay past four, because you don't want to have to unload in the dark. Wolves are bad around the woods back at your place," Bruce warned them.

The other truck pulled off heading in a different direction. Mike pulled back on the road and drove until they found the first store that looked promising.

"What are we going to get here?" Kate asked as they pulled into the parking lot of a Home Depot.

"I need some parts for the tractor, and we can use some gardening tools and water hoses." Mike climbed out of the truck and looked around. There were empty cars everywhere with buggies lying on their sides in every direction.

"Mike? Maybe I should just stay in the truck."

"Nope, you've got to come with me. We don't know who else is out here besides us and Marcus and Bruce. Come on, Kate."

She sighed and climbed out of the truck. She followed Mike up to the storefront where he kicked out the remaining glass to one of the sliding doors. He climbed through then waited on her to do the same.

"Watch for glass, Kate."

He grabbed a cart and handed it to her. "All right let's take each row together. Remember, if you see a wolf, stop and be still. I've got the handgun with me if we need it."

"Are you sure this is a good idea, Mike?" Kate felt like there were a thousand eyes on them now.

"Come on, Kate. It will be fine."

They combed the aisles and loaded up with garden hoses, gloves, and various parts that Mike needed, but there were no other garden implements left. Neither were there any canning supplies. After loading up the camper, they pulled out of the parking lot and followed the road farther into town. The next store they came to was one of those super department stores with everything imaginable inside. Here they found the canning supplies along with some much-needed canned goods and first aid supplies.

Kate grabbed a couple of pairs of insulated underwear for both of them and a pair of boots for her. She figured she needed another pair of jeans, but left most all the other clothes alone. She didn't need them. She had plenty for now.

They loaded up the camper with their finds and decided to make one more stop. They passed by several stores until they came to a sporting goods store. Here they added supplies for the camper and a good winter coat for each of them. There were shells for the rifle, but none for the shotgun or the handgun.

It was close to three now. Kate had just handed the last of the supplies up to Mike to load in the truck when movement caught her attention to the left. She swung her head and nearly screamed. There, not fifteen feet away, stood two wolves.

"Kate, don't move."

"Don't worry, I'm not going to," she whispered back.

They stood there for several long minutes, waiting to see what the wolves were going to do. Kate's legs were beginning to shake. Fear was getting the best of her.

"Mike? I can't stand here much longer. I'm going to start shaking all over."

"Easy, Kate. I've unlocked the doors to the truck. I want you to walk toward the driver's side because it is closer to you. Don't run! Walk slowly. Climb in and crank the truck and pull out of the parking lot."

Kate swallowed around the knot in her throat. She could do this. All she needed to do was walk a few feet ahead. She slowly put one foot in front of the other and took a step forward. The wolves didn't move. She made another step, and they still didn't move. By the time she was within grabbing distance of the door handle, she was soaking wet with sweat and shaking like a leaf. She risked a glance in their direction and nearly cried out. They'd moved closer to her.

"Easy, Kate. Just climb up in the truck. The keys are on the seat. I put them through the back window."

Kate slowly lifted her arm and grabbed the door handle. She opened the door and the wolves started toward her.

"Kate! Get in the fucking truck!"

She climbed in the truck pulling the door closed behind her. She fumbled with the keys, trying to get them in the lock when the first wolf struck the door. Kate screamed and dropped the keys. Mike slid through the sliding window and slammed it shut. They both reached for the keys. Mike came up with them and shoved them in the starter.

"Go, Kate!" She started the truck, slammed it into drive, and floored it.

The wolves chased them all the way out of the parking lot and down the road before they gave up.

"Slow down, Kate, before we have a wreck. It's all right now, Kate. Slow down."

She slowed the truck down and finally stopped in the middle of the road. Her heart was in her throat along with the blasted knot now. She couldn't catch her breath.

"It's okay, Kate. Breathe through your nose so you don't hyperventilate." Mike was the voice of calm, but she'd seen his face turn white, so she knew he'd been as scared as she had been.

"I want to go home, Mike." Kate couldn't unclench her fingers from the steering wheel.

"Change seats with me and we will." He climbed out of the passenger side and walked around to the driver's side and opened the door.

He had to help her unwrap her hands from the wheel then push her over to the other side of the truck. He turned them around toward home, and Kate began to calm down the closer they got to the house. She wasn't sure she would ever be warm again, though. Ice ran through her veins at the realization that they could have been killed. She hadn't even been that scared when she'd nearly been abducted all those times.

As soon as they pulled into the front yard, she climbed out of the cab of the truck and ran inside the house. Mike chuckled behind her.

"Don't you dare laugh at me, Mike Shaw! You could have been killed if you hadn't been able to get through that window when you did."

"It's okay now, Kate. Let's unload so we can get to bed. I'm tired. I know you are, too."

They spent the next two hours unloading everything. It was dark by the time they finished. She let Mike put things up while she fixed them something to eat. After dinner, they each took a quick bath and went straight to bed. Kate lay awake long enough to pray that she wouldn't dream about the wolves. Then she fell into a dreamless sleep.

* * * *

Summer soon turned to fall, and Kate worked from sunup to sundown every day harvesting and canning everything possible. Mike had found a stash of blackberries, and she put up jelly as well as the vegetables from the garden. She fell into bed each night totally exhausted but pleased.

Much to her disdain, though, Mike had made friends with several of the other settlers around the area, including two households of men. Everyone thought they were married, which suited Kate just fine. She wasn't attracted to any of them. If she were interested in anyone it would be Marcus and Bruce, but they were off-limits.

"What do you think about Roy and Evan? They're real hard workers. Their place is in great shape," Mike asked her after he'd been over to borrow their ax for the day.

"No. I don't like them. They're loud and rowdy."

Mike huffed out a breath and walked off without saying anything. Disgust filled her at the thought of any of the men she'd met touching her. She just couldn't see herself with any of them. Mike was quickly losing patience with her, she knew, but she still didn't see why they couldn't continue as they were.

There was a knock at the door. Assuming it would be one of the men her *husband* had befriended, she opened the door to find Bruce standing on the front porch.

"Don't you look before you open a door? How do you know it's not a total stranger?"

"Kate, tell me you didn't just open the door without looking!" Mike stormed into the living room.

"You have people over here all the time. I assumed it was one of them." She frowned at Bruce and stomped off.

She heard the other man warning Mike to teach her to be more careful. She didn't stick around to hear what else he had to say about her. She was pissed because he had been right. She shouldn't have opened the door at all. The other men had warned Mike that strangers had been seen in the area lately.

She busied herself in the kitchen while Mike talked to Bruce out on the front porch. She had no idea what they were talking about, but when Mike returned nearly an hour later, he was smiling.

"What are you so happy about?"

"Bruce and Marcus have cattle. We're going to trade with them for a half a side of beef."

"What are we going to trade?" she asked. She couldn't imagine what they had that the other men didn't.

"They need some of their clothes mended, and I promised you would cook them a full meal."

"You did what?" She couldn't believe he'd bartered her services without asking her.

"Kate, they need their clothes tended to and haven't had a decent cooked meal in years. Since their wife died. We need the meat."

"Fine." She needed to get used to the fact that he was making the decisions. It just irked her not to have any say in anything.

"Bruce said they would drop off some things to be fixed tomorrow. If I'm outside, please be sure it's one of them before you open the door."

"I will. When am I supposed to cook this meal for them?"

"I thought we would have them over at the end of the week. Supposed to start getting cold after that," Bruce said. "We'll need to start getting things ready for the snows." Mike hugged her. "What do you think about them, Kate?"

"They're nice enough, but they're still grieving for their wife."

"I think they've started looking around for another woman now. At least that's the feeling I've gotten when we've talked."

"I'm not going to throw myself on them, so get that out of your head."

"I wouldn't expect you to, Kate."

"Good, because I'm not desperate for a husband. I'm happy like I am."

Mike sighed and shook his head. "You're going to have to choose someone soon, Kate. With these strangers in the area, I'm getting worried."

"I keep the pistol in my reach all the time, Mike. I can shoot what I aim for."

"Yeah, I know, but you might not have time to reach for it. These guys are pretty slick, according to the other men." Mike pursed his lips. "I can't help but be worried, Kate."

"I know, Mike." She sighed. "Just see how things go this winter."

Mike shook his head and headed for his bedroom. Kate finished up in the kitchen and walked to hers. She could see that the worry and strain had aged her brother beyond his twenty-four years. He had lines around his mouth, and he only seemed to smile now when he was around his new friends.

She lay awake in bed a long time, thinking about her plight. Should she pick one of the sets of men and let her brother go? Could she handle being *married* to two men she didn't love? Then she thought about Bruce and Marcus. She was attracted to them, for some reason. Maybe it was because they'd been so careful of her when they'd saved her that day in Barter Town.

Finally, after turning it all around in her head over and over, she fell asleep and dreamed of the two men.

Chapter Five

Saturday night Bruce and Marcus pulled into Mike and Kate's drive and parked behind their truck. Bruce was looking forward to a real home-cooked meal complete with meat and a dessert. He wasn't looking forward to being around Kate when he was attracted to her. It would be hell to handle, but Bruce would enjoy every torturous minute of it. She starred in his dreams each night and was the face he jacked off to each day.

He didn't feel bad about it since she was already married to Mike and there was no chance of there being anything between them. He knew Marcus felt the same way. They'd finally come to grips with the attraction. As long as they didn't act on it, there was nothing wrong with it. At least that is what Bruce told himself.

"Hey, guys. Come on in. Kate has dinner almost ready." Mike had the door open by the time they had gotten out of the truck.

"How are you doing, Mike?" Marcus asked, shaking his hand.

"Fine. We're glad you're here."

They stood in the living area talking until Kate walked into the room wiping her hands on her apron and called them to the table. Bruce could already taste the roast and potatoes. It looked delicious. She'd filled the table full of good things, and he smelled what he thought was blackberry cobbler around it all.

Kate was silent through the meal, but smiled when they told her how good everything was. He could honestly say he hadn't had a meal that good in years. He hated to say it, but even their Irene hadn't cooked anything this good.

When she brought the blackberry cobbler to the table, Bruce figured he'd died and gone to heaven.

"This is the best meal I've had in a very long time," Marcus told her.

"I'm glad you enjoyed it. I have containers so you can take the leftovers home with you for another meal."

"That's mighty thoughtful of you, ma'am," Bruce said.

"Kate, please. I feel old when you call me ma'am."

"Kate. Thanks for fixing our clothes, too. We hated to get new ones when these just needed buttons or a tear sewn up."

"Let's sit in the other room, and you can fill me in on what I need to know about this winter." Mike led them back into the living room.

Bruce watched Kate get up and gather the dishes. He felt like he should help, but followed Mike instead.

They explained about the heavy snows and the need to keep it from piling up against the doors. Mike listened intently to them latching on to every word. *He is so young.* Bruce worried that he was too young to properly take care of Kate, but it wasn't his business.

It wasn't long before they called it a night and said good-bye. They loaded the box of leftovers into the truck and headed home. The sight of Mike and Kate waving them off on the front porch struck him as odd. They weren't hugging, and now that he thought about it, they rarely touched. He shook the thought away as again being none of his business.

Once they had unloaded the food and put it away, they called it a night. Bruce climbed into the shower thinking about Kate and her doe-colored eyes. He could imagine them bright with passion and heavy with desire. His cock had been hard the entire time they'd been there. He had worried that Mike would notice and know that they were thinking about his wife.

The hot water from their gas heater felt good against the evening chill in the house. He quickly cleaned up then sighed at the sight of his cock, still hard as a rock. The damn thing ached he was so hard.

Bruce grasped it at the base of the thick stalk and squeezed then ran his hand up and over the bulbous mushroom head and back down once again. His balls tightened in anticipation. He tugged on his dick as he thought about Kate's luscious red lips. They would stretch wide to accommodate his cock in her mouth.

Bruce wanted to sink his fingers in her hair and hold her still as he pumped his cock into her mouth. She'd moan around him and drive him crazy with the sound. He pulled on his cock a little faster now as his cum began to boil in his balls.

"Fuck." He let it slip out as he thought about her nicely rounded ass and how much he wanted to bury his cock deep in her tight hole.

He pumped his hand up and down his throbbing dick, feeling the burn begin in his spine that let him know he was close. All it took was a few more pulls and thoughts of her swallowing his cock down her throat to send his cum shooting against the shower wall. His ass cheeks clenched as he stood on his toes, feeling as if he would explode.

Bruce caught himself against the ceramic-tiled wall and struggled to catch his breath. His legs were weak, he'd come so hard. The water began to cool, so he quickly cleaned up and shut it off. He pulled on thermals since it was cold in the house. He normally slept nude, but not in the winter. When he climbed into bed, he thought about how it would be to sleep with Kate between him and Marcus.

He shook his head at the thought. It wasn't going to happen, so he needed to stop letting his mind think about it.

He lay there for over an hour trying to think of something besides how much he wanted to fuck Mike's wife or watch Marcus fuck her. Finally, he gave in and let himself sink into an erotic dream that starred Kate.

* * * *

Kate finished washing clothes and set them aside so she could rest for a few minutes before she went outside to hang them up. Mike had warned her they probably only had another couple of days of sun before the snow set in. Hard to believe it would snow considering it was still fairly nice during the day. Yes, it got cold at night, but not unbearably cold.

Mike was out turning the garden one last time. He promised to be in by lunchtime. She had soup ready to warm up on the stove. She knew better than to trust his sense of time.

As she picked up the clothes to hang out, her mind wandered toward their neighbors, Marcus and Bruce. They had been perfect gentlemen the night before and had honestly seemed to enjoy her meal. She was glad. They had been good to them and a wealth of knowledge for Mike. It didn't hurt that they were easy to look at either. Both men were big, but not overly so. She bet their wife had been well cared for.

She frowned. Where had that thought come from? *You don't need to be thinking like that about them. They're still in mourning for her.* She smiled at the idea someone would ever love her enough to mourn for her for two years.

Kate set the tub with the wet clothes on the table under the clothesline and began hanging clothes on the line. She thought she heard something behind her, but when she turned to look, there was nothing there. She fingered the gun in the pocket of her jacket.

Finally, she turned back around and went back to work with the clothes. Suddenly someone grabbed her from behind, slapping a hand over her mouth. She struggled, but couldn't get her hand to her pocket to get at the gun. A man walked around in front of her and smiled.

"Looks like we've got us a keeper, Jim. She's a little plump, but that just makes her healthy."

The one holding her chuckled with his face against the side of hers. She shoved her head back and hit him in the chin. He cursed and jerked her back against him. The other man just laughed.

"You do that again, woman, and I'm going to make you wish you hadn't."

The man holding her relaxed his grip on her mouth, and she bit him then screamed when he let go of her.

"Fucking bitch!" He turned her around and backhanded her across the face. It knocked her to the ground.

She scrambled to get away, but both men were on her in an instant. Then one of the men was pulled off of her. She fought the one still holding her and saw Mike fighting the first man. He was so much bigger than Mike. Kate was scared for him. Then she was too busy fighting the second man to watch Mike.

She could hear the sounds of fists hitting flesh, but she didn't know who was winning. Instead, she was busy trying to keep the second man from choking her and reaching for her gun at the same time.

The second man made the mistake of thinking he'd subdued her and pulled back. She used the opportunity to reach for the gun only to hear the deafening sound of another gun going off. She turned just in time to see Mike grab his chest and sink to the ground.

"No!" she screamed.

The first man aimed to shoot him again, but Kate had her gun out and fired almost in the same motion. The other man dropped his gun and sank to his knees. Blood blossomed from his lower chest. She fired again and again before the second man managed to wrestle the gun from her. He stuck it in his pants and slapped her.

"He's dead, you bitch! I'll make you sorry you were ever born." He grabbed her by the hair and pulled her to her feet. Then he slammed her against the side of the house.

Suddenly the sound of hoofbeats could be heard despite the roaring from the gun in her ears. The man jerked his head around and pulled her gun from his pants pointing it in the general direction the sound was coming from.

Marcus and Bruce appeared out of the woods riding horses. She grabbed the man's hand and bit his shoulder to keep him from aiming at the two men. He yelped and turned around to hit her, but there was another gunshot. He grabbed his arm and turned around to face Bruce.

Kate didn't stop to see what happened next. She ran for Mike. He was bleeding but alive. She held her hands over the wound to his upper chest in an effort to stop the bleeding. Then Marcus was there pulling her off of him.

"Move and let me see about him, Kate. I'll take care of him." Marcus tore open Mike's shirt to look at the wound then he stuffed the shirt over it and pressed down.

Kate couldn't stop the tears as she kissed Mike's forehead then settled his head in her lap.

"Marcus?" Bruce hurried over to them. "How is he?"

"He's alive. He's been beaten up pretty thoroughly, though. We need to get the bullet out so we can stop the bleeding."

"Please, you've got to help him. Please don't let him die."

"Kate, calm down and look at me." Bruce turned her toward him.

She had a difficult time seeing him through her tears.

"We need to move him to our place because we have everything we need there to help him. I need your help though, so you've got to be calm and do what I say. Can you do that?" Bruce held her shoulders in his big hands.

Kate swallowed hard and nodded her head up and down. "What do I need to do?"

"Where are the keys to the truck?" he asked.

"In his pocket, I'm sure."

Bruce searched carefully through Mike's pockets and pulled out a set of keys.

"I'm going to go get the truck and bring it around here. I need you to go get blankets and a pillow out of the house and come right back here with them."

Kate nodded and sprinted for the house. She grabbed the blanket off the couch then another one along with her pillow. She grabbed them off Mike's bed because it was closer. She raced back outside in time to see Bruce pulling back around with the truck. He stopped not far from where Mike and Marcus were. She stood trembling from head to foot, holding the blankets and pillow.

Bruce opened the back door and grabbed one of the blankets. He doubled it and laid it across the seat then added the pillow.

"Hold on to the blanket until we get him in there. Then you're going to wrap it around both of you so you can hold pressure on his wound. Got it?" He stared at her. There was compassion in his eyes.

"I'll hold pressure on his wound," she repeated.

"Good. Marcus? Are you ready?" Bruce helped Marcus pick Mike up and lay him in the back seat. "Now get in the floorboard and wrap the cover around you both and hold pressure."

Kate was already in the truck and wrapping the covers around them when Marcus climbed in the cab and put the truck in gear.

"Where are you going?" she asked Bruce.

"I'm going to be right behind you with the horses. I can't leave them here."

Kate only nodded and turned her attention back to Mike. The ride to their place seemed to take forever. She winced at every bump in the road. Mike seemed oblivious to it all, though, thank God.

Please, God, let him be okay. I don't know what I'll do without him. Kate prayed the entire trip. When they finally rolled to a stop, she breathed a sigh of relief and waited for one of the men to come get them. The door opened and Marcus climbed in next to her.

"Let me see how he's doing."

Kate moved back and waited for Marcus to check on him before he nodded for her to return to holding pressure.

Bruce stuck his head inside. "I'm going to pull the saddles and let the horses go in the barn. I'll be right there to help you."

"I'm going to put him on the kitchen table to cut out the bullet. I'll need you for that." Marcus began pulling Mike out of the truck.

Kate held Mike's head until Marcus could pick him up and carry him to the house.

"Run up ahead and open the door. It's not locked."

Kate pulled up the blanket and ran for the door. She opened it wide and stood back while Marcus carried Mike through it and on into the kitchen. He laid Mike on the big wooden table and began pulling off the rest of his shirt. She wrung her hands, unsure what to do.

"Hold pressure while I round up everything I need, Kate. Talk to him and tell him to hold on." Marcus squeezed her arm then disappeared into the other room.

"Come on, Mike. Hold on for me. I can't do this without you, Mike. Please, don't die on me." Tears continued to roll down her cheeks.

Bruce hurried in through the back door. He looked at her then went to the sink and filled a boiler with water and sat it on the stove. He turned it on then returned to the sink and washed his hands.

"How's he doing over there, Kate?" he asked as he carefully cleaned his hands and forearms.

"I don't know. God, he's so pale." She sniffed, trying to keep from breaking down.

"Hang on, Kate. We're going to do everything we can for him." Bruce dried his hands on a clean towel then walked over and began washing off Mike's chest with a cloth he had soaked in the hot water from the sink.

"I'm so scared, Bruce. He's all I have."

"I know. Just keep holding pressure while I clean around you."

Marcus walked in with a box, which he sat on one of the chairs. He took out a few things and dumped them in the boiler on the stove. Then he began cleaning Mike's chest with iodine.

"Kate, look at me." Bruce turned her head from staring at Mike. "I need you to look at me and concentrate."

She swallowed and nodded, looking at him now. He held her shoulders in his big hands and smiled. He had a nice one when he did. He just didn't seem to do it much.

"We're going to have to cut the bullet out of his shoulder to stop the bleeding so he can get better. It's going to be rough. If you don't think you can handle it, go in the living room and wrap up on the couch until we finish."

"I'm not leaving him," she said, shaking her head.

"Then you have to stay out of the way no matter what happens. We can't take care of him and you, too. Understand?"

"Kate?" Mike's weak voice reached her.

She pushed around Bruce and went to Mike.

"Mike. Oh, God. You're hurt bad, Mike."

"I know, Kate. You'll be okay, though."

"I'm fine. Bruce and Marcus are going to take care of you. You'll be fine, Mike. You've got to be fine." She cupped his cheek in her hand. She couldn't stop the tears from falling.

"Bruce?" Mike looked toward the other man.

"Yeah, Mike. I'm right here.

"Get my wallet out of my pocket."

"We can do that later, man," Bruce said.

"No, Got to now. Might not be able to later."

Bruce reached under him and pulled out his wallet.

"Inside are Kate's papers. Take them. Giving her to you. Take care of her."

"What papers? What are you talking about, Mike?" Kate stared at the folded-up papers in Bruce's hand.

"Kate isn't my wife. She's my sister." Mike was panting now.

"We can talk about it later, Mike. Rest now." Bruce didn't open the folded papers.

"Mike?" Kate couldn't believe what he had done. "What are you doing?"

"Kate, later. Mike, drink this." Marcus raised Mike's head and gave him a bottle of whiskey to drink.

Kate just shook her head and stepped back. Bruce grabbed her when she would have fallen. He held her for a second then helped her sit down on one of the kitchen chairs.

"Kate. Don't think about it right now. First we have to take care of Mike." He stuffed the papers into his pocket and turned to help Marcus.

Kate couldn't help but think about it. Her brother had had papers drawn up on her to give her to someone. He had made her a piece of property, and he was holding the papers to her life. She never would have believed he would do something like that. She watched him close his eyes and fall asleep.

Chapter Six

Bruce helped Marcus operate on Mike, praying the man would make it. If he didn't, he wasn't sure how Kate would do. Hell, he was still in shock to find out they weren't married, but brother and sister.

Marcus finally finished the last stitch and covered the wound with a gauze dressing and tape. He wiped the sweat off his forehead with his sleeve and looked at Bruce. They each looked over at where Kate sat staring into space. She was in shock.

"I'll sit with him for the first few hours," Bruce said. "You get cleaned up and get some sleep. Take Kate with you. She needs to rest."

"No, I'll take the first watch. You take care of Kate. I want to monitor him for a couple of hours. Then I'll come wake you up." Marcus walked over to the sink and began cleaning up.

Bruce sighed. He walked over to where Kate sat and knelt in front of her.

"Kate. Let's go get some rest, baby. He's sleeping now, and Marcus is going to watch him."

"I'm not leaving him. I'll watch him."

"No. You need to get some rest so you can help us with him tomorrow when he wakes up. He's going to be in pain and will probably run a fever. We'll have to keep him sponged off. I'll need your help with that."

"I don't want to leave him. He might not—he might not wake up," she finally whispered.

"He's going to wake up, Kate. We're going to get you cleaned so you can rest. You can sit with him tomorrow. Come on." He stood up and held out his hand for her.

Kate looked at it then up at him. She drew in a deep breath and took his hand, letting him draw her to her feet. She stopped to kiss Mike's cheek then continued to follow Bruce out of the kitchen and up the stairs. He led her to the master bedroom and closed the door.

"I'm going to run you a bath, Kate. You'll feel better once you've cleaned up." She just nodded and stood in the middle of the bedroom floor. "Why don't you go ahead and get out of those dirty clothes?"

He left her there and hurried into the bathroom to run the bathwater for her. She was in shock. Bruce figured that too much had happened to her. Between being attacked, seeing her brother shot, finding out he'd had papers drawn up on her, and watching him operated on, she was on overload. He would be lucky if she didn't pass out on him. Bruce shook his head and watched the water creep up in the tub.

When he finished running the water, he walked out of the bathroom to find her still standing in the same place without having gotten undressed. He sighed and walked over to her. She looked up when he stood in front of her.

"Let's get you undressed and in the tub, Kate." He pulled off her jacket then started to pull off her T-shirt when she suddenly came to herself.

"What are you doing?"

"Getting you undressed and into the tub." He pulled the shirt over her head.

Kate crossed her arms over her bra. "I can undress myself."

"Okay. You get undressed and into the tub. I'll go get you something to wear to bed."

Kate nodded and hurried into the bathroom, shutting the door behind her. Bruce was glad he didn't hear the door lock. He walked down to his room and searched through his things until he found an old button-down shirt that would cover her to her knees. He didn't have anything else that would fit her lower half. Everything would fall off.

He walked back downstairs to check on Mike. Marcus was putting away the last of the supplies. He'd transferred Mike to the couch and had drawn up a kitchen chair by it.

"How's he doing?"

"Holding his own is about all I can say. It's not good, though. He was beaten pretty bad as well as shot. I think he has a couple of broken ribs. If he gets pneumonia, he's gone."

Bruce nodded. "Kate's in the bathtub. She's in shock."

"I'm not surprised. Man, can you believe it? She's not married to him. They're brother and sister."

"Yeah." He remembered the papers in his pocket. He pulled them out and unfolded them.

"Looks like ownership papers all right," Marcus said, looking over his shoulder at them.

"I'll be damned. He had already filled in our names. He was planning on giving her to us all along." Bruce blew out a breath. "Fuck."

"Why do you suppose he chose us to take her?"

"I'd say he realized he couldn't take care of her by himself anymore and figured we were decent enough men. I can't believe he didn't choose one of the others, though. They are closer to her age, I'm sure." Bruce folded up the papers and carefully placed them in his wallet.

"Get some rest, Bruce. I have a feeling we're in for a long few days keeping Mike alive." Marcus sat down on the chair next to the couch.

"Wake me up in a couple of hours. Try to keep from waking Kate up, though. Getting her to go to sleep is going to be tough."

Bruce walked back upstairs and knocked on the bathroom door.

"Who is it?"

"It's me, Kate. I have something for you to wear."

"Just leave it on the bed and I'll get it."

"Come on out, Kate. I'm not going anywhere. I'm going to take a shower when you get out."

Kate slowly opened the door, holding a towel around her. She held out one hand toward him. Bruce smiled and handed her the shirt. She closed the door back. He heard her moving around in the other room. Finally, the door opened again and she walked out wearing his old flannel shirt. He had been right. It came down to her knees, though the sides were rounded and showed a good bit of thigh.

"Climb on into bed. I'll cover you with the extra blanket." He held up the sheets.

She hurried under the covers and watched as he added the extra blanket. She still looked cold, but he'd be out of the shower soon enough and warm her up. He almost smiled. That was going to be a fight, he was sure. She would balk at sleeping with him.

He walked into the bathroom and quickly stripped before stepping into the shower. He had brought another pair of thermal bottoms to sleep in. As soon as he had cleaned up and dried off, he stepped into them. He walked out of the bathroom and headed for the bed. When he nudged her with his hand to get her to scoot over some, her eyes flew open and she yelped.

"What are you doing?"

"Getting into bed. Scoot over."

"You're not sleeping with me!" She tightened her hold on the covers.

"Listen, Kate. It's going to get very cold in here in another couple of hours when the sun goes down. You can't sleep in this bed alone. All we're going to do is sleep. I need to rest before Marcus comes in and wakes me up to watch Mike for a few hours while he sleeps. It's going to take all of us over the next few days to keep your brother alive. Do you understand? You've got to rest while you can, Kate."

"I understand, but I don't know you," she whispered, near tears again.

"Just sleep, Kate. That's all."

She stared up at him for several seconds then slowly backed across the bed to let him climb in.

"You're getting the spot I already warmed up," she complained.

Bruce chuckled and pulled her over almost on top of him. "Lay your head on my shoulder and go to sleep, Kate."

She lay stiff as a board for a long time before she finally relaxed and fell asleep. Bruce ran his hand lightly over her hair and curled his fingers in it. He couldn't believe she was there in the bed with him, in his arms. His cock knew it, though. He sighed. If she woke up and felt his dick pushing against her belly, she would scream bloody murder.

Bruce drew in her scent and rested his chin against the top of her head. She felt so right there next lying on him. He stiffened his jaw. He wasn't going to let himself fall in love, though. It hurt too much when the one you loved was gone. And they always left. Either voluntarily or through death. His mother had left. His first wife had left. Then Irene had been killed. No, it was better if he didn't take that step again.

He breathed in her essence once again and let himself drift into sleep.

* * * *

Marcus stood up and stretched. It was time to wake up Bruce and let him take his place watching over Mike. So far the man was alive and holding his own, barely. He was running a low-grade fever, but nothing major so far. The last time he had checked the wound and changed the dressing, it looked pretty good. If he could make it through the next twelve hours, he had a fighting chance.

He walked into the kitchen and put on a pot of coffee for Bruce. He would need it to wake up and stay awake for the next four or five hours. Marcus was looking forward to climbing into bed. Not just for the sleep, but also because it meant being near Kate. His cock stirred. Fuck! He couldn't think about her without his dick getting ideas.

He poured a cup of coffee and, after looking in on Mike one last time, carried the coffee upstairs to wake Bruce. When he walked into the bedroom, it was to find Kate burrowed into his brother's side like a little rabbit, seeking the warmth of his body. Marcus looked relaxed and at peace for the first time in a long time. Kate would be good for them if they could convince her they would take good care of her.

Despite her brother having given her to them, neither of them would take her without her agreement. They didn't force women to share their bed. Seduce, though, was a different matter. If she could be seduced, they would figure out how.

She was lovely to look at lying there wrapped up in his brother. From her honey-blonde hair to her gently rounded belly to the flare of her plump hips, she exuded sex appeal, and she didn't even know it. That was part of her allure. She had no idea how beautiful she was to them. God knows they had tried to keep their attraction a secret since they had thought she was married. Now, knowing otherwise, they were free to make it known to her.

Marcus moved further into the room and sat the coffee cup on the bedside table on Bruce's side. He leaned in and whispered to the other man.

"Bruce? Wake up. Coffee's on."

Bruce woke without moving a muscle other than his eyelids. He looked up to see Marcus squatting next to the bed and sniffed the air. He started to roll out then realized he had someone next to him. Confusion crossed his face then was gone in an instant, almost as if it were never there.

"Move slowly and she might not wake up," Marcus suggested.

Bruce drew in a deep breath and slowly extracted himself from her body before climbing out of the bed. They both held their breath as Kate's face wrinkled up as if unsure what was going on. Then she settled back down without opening her eyes. Her breathing slowly evened out once again.

Bruce zeroed in on the coffee and took a sip.

"How's he doing?"

"Holding his own. Has a low-grade fever, but nothing to worry about just yet." Marcus began undressing. He needed a shower.

"I'll keep watch. If he starts spiking a good one, I'll start sponging him down." Bruce took another sip of the coffee then sat it down to get dressed.

"I'm heading for a shower. Wake me up if you think he's getting bad."

"Will do."

Marcus padded naked into the bathroom and closed the door so as not to wake up Kate. She needed as much sleep as she could get to deal with whatever the next day brought. If they were lucky, it would be a recovering Mike. If they weren't…well, they had done their best for her and him both.

Marcus turned on the shower and adjusted the water to a bearable temperature. When he stepped in beneath the spray, he sighed. Crusted blood from hours before began to soften and sluice away. He lathered up and scrubbed to make sure he got rid of it all. Rinsing off, he thought about Kate and what having her there with them could mean. Bruce was taken with her despite his denial over the past months. It was evident in the way he had treated her since they had saved her and, hopefully, Mike from their attackers.

Yeah, Bruce would bond with her. He just didn't know if he would let himself love her. Marcus had been too young to remember their mother leaving them with their abusive drunk of a father. Then his first wife had left him for another man. He had said when Irene had been killed that he would never let another woman have his heart just to crush it when she left.

Bruce started to get out of the shower, but he realized he still had an erection that would get in the way of sleeping. If Kate were to wake up and see his throbbing cock, she would probably run screaming from the bedroom. No, he needed to take care of it first.

He lathered his hands with soap for lubrication and ran his hand down the length of his dick before squeezing and sliding back up again. He thumbed the rim of the mushroom head then ran the palm of his hand over the top and squeezed his way back down again. His cock ached for the warmth of woman to sink into instead of merely his hand.

He pumped his cock with a firm grip, thinking of Kate's mouth stretched wide around his cock. Her plump lips would be swollen from his kisses as she swallowed his dick, taking him to the back of her throat.

The warm water rolled down his back as electrical impulses gathered at the base of his spine. He pulled faster as he imagined Kate letting him hold her head while he face fucked her. She would trust him not to hurt her. He never would. He could see her eyes dark with arousal as he thrust his cock in and out of her wet mouth. Marcus's balls began to draw up as he grew closer to climaxing. He reached between his legs and cupped them in his hand.

Faster and tighter, he tugged on his dick, imagining now sinking into her tight cunt over and over again. Fire burned down his spine and ignited his balls. Cum boiled in them as he pumped his hand up and down his cock.

Just as he imagined shooting his seed inside of Kate's hot cunt, he erupted, cum shooting from his dick to the floor below. He threw out a hand to catch himself against the shower wall.

"Fuck."

He cleaned up and got out of the now cooling shower to dry off on shaky legs. If he came that hard just thinking about her, God only knew how hard he'd come once he was inside of her. His ass cheeks were sore from squeezing as he came.

Once he had his breathing under control, Marcus eased out of the bathroom into the bedroom in hopes of not waking Kate up before he was in the bed with her. He pulled on a pair of thermal underwear knowing she would balk at having a completely naked man in bed with her. Marcus slid beneath the sheets and backed up to her. She instantly sought his warmth and snuggled to his back. He briefly thought of turning over and pulling her into his arms, but he dismissed that thought, figuring she would wake up.

The feel of her breasts mashed against his back stirred his cock once again. He nearly moaned out loud at the thing noticing. He was going to end up with a fucking hard-on after all. Then he grinned. The fact that she aroused him so easily was good. He only hoped that one day she would be aroused by them just as easily.

Marcus settled down and let sleep take him. He knew things were bound to be rough over the next few days. He wanted to be ready for whatever happened.

Chapter Seven

Something tickled Kate's nose. She twitched it, but it didn't go away. She brushed at it and found her hand against something warm and hairy. Instantly her eyes opened and focused on the fact that she was nearly on top of Marcus's chest. She panicked and started to move. Hands came out and held her still.

"Easy, Kate. Your knee is in a very tender spot right now," Marcus said in a tight voice.

"Oh. Um, what do I do?" She registered that her knee was squashed up against his balls. *Thank God he has on underwear.*

"Just ease back. Then you can move. Just don't put any pressure on that knee until you've moved back." Marcus slowly let go of her arms.

Kate slipped her leg back and then pulled herself off of his chest. She had basically crawled on top of the poor man. It was a wonder he had been able to breathe. The intimacy of their positions wasn't lost on her. She just hoped he didn't get any ideas. God knew she had grown wet thinking about how close they had been.

That thought went right out the window when he threw off the covers and stood up beside the bed. He held out his hand to help her up. There, standing out in front of him against the thermal pants in all its pride and glory, was the largest cock she'd ever seen. Well, not seen exactly since it was covered, but damn it was big. She blushed at the realization that she had been staring at it. She risked a glance up and sure enough Marcus had noticed by the lopsided grin on his face.

Kate scowled at him and marched into the bathroom ahead of him. She was sure he had wanted it first, but she wasn't going to stand around waiting on him to gawk at her less-than-decent attire.

"Kate, I'll leave something for you to wear on the bed once I've gotten dressed."

"Um, thanks. That would be good," she managed to get out around the knot in her throat.

She took her time in the bathroom making sure to give Marcus plenty of time to come back and leave whatever he planned before she ventured outside the bathroom. She didn't want to run into him again without being fully clothed. God, she had slept with both him and Bruce in next to nothing. She shivered at the thought. Part of her could acknowledge that she had enjoyed it, but the other part of her was appalled at her attraction to them.

She cracked the bathroom door and snuck a peek to see if the promised clothes were waiting on her. Sure enough, a pair of sweatpants and a sweatshirt lay across the foot of the bed. There was no sign of Marcus or Bruce, so she hurried out of the bathroom and changed clothes. The sweatpants were much too long, but she was able to roll up the legs so she wouldn't trip and fall. She did the same thing to the sleeves. She had to pull the ties on the warm-ups extra tight to keep them up.

Satisfied with her appearance, she quickly made the bed and took the stairs down to the living room where Mike was on the couch in front of a roaring fire. He looked pale and gaunt in the flickering light.

Kate rushed over to kneel by his side. She looked up at Bruce in hopes he would have some good news.

"He hasn't woken up all night, Kate. He's running a fever, but so far, it isn't serious. His wound has some redness around it, so I'm worried it's getting infected." Bruce's lips thinned when she bit her lower lip.

"How high has his fever gotten?" she asked.

"Just one hundred so far. I'm keeping a close watch on it."

"What can I do to help?" She wanted to do something. Sitting around watching him would drive her crazy.

"Kate, if you want to help, you could fix us something for breakfast," Bruce suggested.

"Cook? Um, sure. I can do that." She took one last look at Mike and brushed a kiss on his warm forehead then walked out of the living room into the kitchen.

She poured a cup of the coffee and sipped at it while she searched to see what the men had available to cook. The coffee was a bit strong, but she felt she needed it to deal with the two men who her brother had given her to.

That thought tightened her gut and things further south. Her pussy leaked a small amount of her arousal. She couldn't help but be attracted to them. They'd saved her not just once, but twice, and were two of the most ruggedly handsome men she had ever met. Her inner desire to know them more intimately had been a fantasy. Now, it could very easily become a reality if Mike didn't recover.

He had to get well. She couldn't imagine life without her brother in it. He'd been her mainstay for years now. Once he was well, things would go back to how they had been. Yet deep down inside, she knew that wasn't possible. Yesterday had only proved that he couldn't keep her safe by himself. Fear threatened to overwhelm her as she tried to push the thoughts back for the time being. She needed to cook something for them for breakfast. They were taking care of Mike and deserved a filling meal.

Kate settled on deer steak with gravy. She was just about to start cooking when Marcus walked into the kitchen. He smiled at her and grabbed a basket and a bucket.

"I'm going to go milk the cow and grab whatever eggs I can find from the hens if you want to wait for me to come back."

"You have hens and a milk cow?" She could cook them eggs to go with the steak.

"Yep. I'll be back in a little while. Hold off for about thirty minutes." He pulled on his coat and slipped his feet into a pair of boots standing at the back door.

Then he slipped outside, letting a swirl of cold air in to circulate around the kitchen. Kate shivered and wrapped her arms around herself. She sipped on the coffee and thought about what her future would hold even if Mike recovered. He would insist that she had to find two men. Even if these two didn't want her, he would surely pick one of the other two sets of bachelors in the area.

Neither of them were the least bit attractive to her. They all seemed so young, when in fact they were about the same age she was. If she was going to be honest, she would have to admit that she was attracted to Bruce and Marcus. They aroused more than just a curiosity about them. They left her wet when they touched her or talked to her. She'd felt scandalous thinking about them when they were obviously grieving over their late wife.

The back door opened, startling her. She looked up and found Marcus struggling to shut the door with a basket in one hand and a bucket nearly full of milk with the other hand. She raced to the door and pushed it shut against the wind.

"Getting colder outside. I expect it's going to snow soon. Got to get over to your place and do something about the mess we left behind."

"Oh, I hadn't thought about that." She shivered at the memory of the two men.

"Fuck! I'm sorry I brought that up, Kate."

"It's okay. I'm going to have breakfast ready in just a few minutes."

She busied herself at the stove, still keenly aware of the other man in the room. He strained the milk and then left it covered by the back door where the cool air seeped beneath it.

Kate quickly filled two plates with deer steak, gravy, and eggs. She carried them into the other room for the men then returned with fresh coffee.

"Do you want a glass of milk? I didn't think of that." She clasped her hands in front of her.

"No thanks, Kate." Bruce waved toward the kitchen. "Go fix your plate and come sit down and eat."

"I ate while I cooked. I can watch Mike while you eat."

"That would be good. We'll go on into the kitchen, then." Bruce stood up and Marcus followed him.

Kate took Mike's hand in hers and squeezed it. She leaned over close to his ear and talked to him.

"Fight, Mike. You've got to fight for me. I can't deal with life all alone. Don't leave me like this." She squeezed his hand and waited in hopes he would squeeze back, but his hand remained flaccid in hers.

She checked his forehead several times to find it slightly hotter to her. She took the thermometer she found on the table by the couch and placed it under his arm. When she pulled it out several minutes later, it read 101.4. She shook it down and replaced it in its holder on the table.

Marcus walked in as she stood up to go get them.

"What is it?" he asked. He seemed to be aware that something was wrong.

"His temperature is up." She told him what it was.

"Damn, I was afraid of this. He's getting an infection. Without antibiotics, we're just going to have to sweat it out of him and hope it will work."

"I don't want him to die, Marcus." Kate felt the tears well up in her eyes.

"I know. We're going to do everything we can to keep him alive." He ran his hand down her arm. "Why don't you sit with him for a while and monitor his temperature while I clean up the kitchen."

"Where is Bruce?"

"He's gone to your place to take care of things. He'll be back in a few hours." Marcus moved the chair closer to where Mike lay on the couch and urged Kate to sit down. "I'll just be in the kitchen if you need me."

Kate nodded without looking at him. She hated for anyone to see her cry, and it seemed she had cried a lot around them. Once he was gone, she took a damp cloth and bathed Mike's forehead and face. The fire continued to radiate enough heat that she was hot, but knew it was for Mike's benefit that they kept it built up. One of them had draped several blankets over him as well.

Nearly an hour later, Marcus came in and suggested she get up and walk around some while he checked over their patient. Kate got up and moved around the living room for a few seconds, but drifted back to watch Marcus check her brother's wound and dressing. The skin around the stitches was puckered and an angry red. He cleaned the area with alcohol and covered it with a new dressing of gauze and tape.

"Help me turn him a little, Kate. We don't want him to end up with pneumonia if we can help it." Together they turned him farther on his side.

Mike immediately began coughing some. Kate rubbed his back in circles, hoping he would be okay. When he settled down again, she sat back on the chair and bathed his face and neck with the cool, damp cloth.

Several hours later, Bruce returned, looking haggard and exhausted. He carried two suitcases with him.

"I packed up some of yours and Mike's clothes so you'll be comfortable while you're here," he said by way of explanation. "I'll stick them in the bedroom for you to unpack when you get ready to get to them."

"Thanks, that was really thoughtful of you. I know you have to be exhausted. You've been up for at least twelve hours, I'm sure."

"I'm fine. I'll head to bed after dinner. I'm going to shower now. Where's Marcus?" Bruce frowned.

"Upstairs doing something. I'm not sure what."

"How's Mike doing?"

"His wound's infected and he's running a higher temperature, but it hasn't gone any higher since this morning." Kate attempted a smile.

"Good. I'll send Marcus down to relive you so maybe you could fix us something to eat." Bruce turned and headed for the stairs.

Kate couldn't help but smile at the fact that she had become the cook for them. No doubt they preferred her cooking over theirs. She figured she preferred hers over theirs as well. She had learned to cook at her mother's knee from the time she was ten and able to follow directions. She missed her mom and all the valuable lessons she'd taught Kate. Times like these, she could use her mom's advice on what she should do.

"Kate, I'm back. You can go see what you can rustle up for dinner." Marcus laid a hand on her shoulder.

"Okay. There's no change. I'm just washing his face and neck with the wet cloth."

"Let's turn him again before you go."

They rolled him to his other side so that his back faced the fire and his face the back of the couch. Kate arranged a pillow to help keep him propped so he wouldn't roll off the couch.

Dinner proved to be a quiet affair with Marcus eating while watching Mike. She and Bruce ate at the table. Both men had seconds while Kate barely managed to eat half of her meal.

Worry over Mike's condition stole her appetite.

Bruce helped her clean up the kitchen. She wasn't used to having help and told him she could handle it by herself, but he insisted, so she kept her mouth shut.

Around nine that night, Bruce came in and roused her from her chair next to Mike.

"I know it's early, but we need our rest with the way we're watching your brother. Let's go get some sleep, Kate. Marcus will wake me up to relive him around two in the morning. You need your rest as well." He took her hand and pulled her to her feet.

Marcus walked in, and before she knew what to expect, he hugged her and kissed her on the forehead.

"Sleep well, Kate. I'll see you in the morning."

"'Night, Marcus. Wake me up if there's any change in him, okay?" She begged him with her eyes.

"I will, Kate. You and Bruce get some rest." Marcus gave her a little shove toward Bruce then took her chair and sat down.

Chapter Eight

Relived of her nursing duties, there was nothing she could do but follow Bruce upstairs. He opened the door to the bedroom then closed it behind them to keep in any heat they generated. Without the fireplace, they were dependent on each other and the mountain of covers that were piled on the bed. She felt much more comfortable with the covers than her bedmate.

"We can shower together. That way we both get hot water. Plus, there won't be any cooling off in the bathroom when we open and close the door for each other." Bruce strode toward the bathroom carrying a pair of warm-ups. "Grab your sleep clothes and come on, Kate."

"I don't mind taking a shower after you," she said, rummaging through the suitcase he had packed. It was surprisingly neat, and he'd been thorough. Everything she might need seemed to be there.

"You don't have to shower with me, Kate, but Marcus and I are your men now. Your brother signed you over to us even before this happened."

Kate's gasp sounded loud in the quiet of the room. "What are you talking about?"

Bruce's lips grew thin, but he pulled out his wallet then extracted the papers Mike had given him the day before. He spread them out and handed them to Kate. She read over them and upon seeing their names in her brother's handwriting, she knew she was lost. With shaking hands, she handed the papers back to Bruce and slowly began taking off her clothes in the chilly bedroom.

"Kate, if you don't want to do this, it's okay. You've had a lot to deal with in the last twenty-four hours."

She continued removing her clothes despite his assurance that she didn't have to.

"Not here, Kate. It will be warmer in the bathroom. Come on. Bring your nightclothes." Bruce gently took her arm and propelled her into the bathroom where he closed the door and began stripping.

Kate turned her back and took off her clothes in a near state of shock. Her brother really had given her away. He hadn't waited for her to pick anyone, but made up her mind for her. What if she had picked one of the other pairs of men? What would he have done then? She slipped out of the warm-ups then carefully folded them before removing the sweatshirt. She folded it as well.

The water in the shower came on behind her, and she heard Bruce shuffling around as he adjusted the water temperature. She hugged herself in an effort to ward off the cold inside of her more so than the chill in the air.

A soft haze of fog drifted across the top of the bathroom as the shower warmed the room. Once again she thought about the fact that her brother had given her to them. How could she live with these two men that she barely knew? She swallowed down the bitter taste of worry and made up her mind. She was attracted to them. They had been nothing but kind to her. She could do much worse.

"Climb in, Kate. The water is warm enough now." Bruce stood totally nude just inside the shower stall. He held out his hand.

She swallowed and without looking at anything below the waist, she let him lead her into the shower's spray. He circled her around behind him so that the water didn't beat down on her face. She reached for the cloth he held in his hands, but he held it above her head and soaped it.

"I'll bathe you, Kate. Just relax and let me take care of you tonight." His deep rich voice vibrated across her body like strings on a violin.

"I can bathe myself, Bruce. You don't have to do that."

"I want to bathe you, Kate. If you'll let me."

"If you're sure that you want to."

"Do you want me to, Kate?"

She swallowed around the weakening fear in her throat and nodded. She concentrated on a spot just below his chin but no lower than his shoulders. When he began lathering her shoulders and neck, he stood close to her. Close enough that his cock brushed against her belly. She drew in a swift breath and swallowed hard again to keep from moving away from him. She tilted her head a little in defiance because she wasn't a coward. Not really.

"Easy, Kate. I'm not going to hurt you. Neither Marcus or myself will ever hurt you, baby. I promise." Bruce continued to soap her up.

He turned her to face the back of the shower and rubbed the cloth around her shoulders and down her back. When he reached her ass, he continued to bathe her as if he had done it a million times before. She felt the heat rise in her neck and face as he cleaned between her legs then on down her thighs until he reached her feet. When he moved away from the spray so that it would rinse her, she had to quickly look up to avoid staring at his engorged cock.

Something tightened deep within her body at the glimpse she got despite her good intentions not to look. He slipped back between the shower and her body once again. This time he turned her so he could bathe her front. She grabbed his wrist when he started on her breasts.

"Really, Bruce. I can do it." Her voice quivered despite her resolve to not show how nervous he made her.

"Let me, baby." He looked deep in her eyes until she slowly dropped her hands.

Bruce quickly bathed her body but instead of letting the shower rinse her this time, he hung the cloth on a rod and slowly began to massage her shoulders, slick with soapy water. He moved to her chest where he slowly lowered to encompass her breasts. He mounded them with his hands then concentrated on her nipples, flicking and rubbing them until she moaned out loud. She was appalled that the sound had come from her mouth, but couldn't stop it. She couldn't stop anything he was doing, because a part of her didn't want him to stop.

Kate cringed at that part of her. It betrayed her. She shouldn't want anything to do with either him or Marcus, but deep inside, she wanted to feel their flesh next to hers. She wanted to feel their flesh inside of hers.

Shivering, her knees nearly buckled when he reached her mound with his questing hand. He easily held her up as he explored her pussy with his fingers. The more he stimulated her, the tighter her body wound in an uneasy anticipation of something she wasn't sure she wanted, but knew she couldn't do without.

"Easy, baby. Don't fall." He wrapped an arm around her and turned her around in the shower to rinse her free of the soap. Then he slowly lowered her to the shower floor as he quickly bathed and rinsed off.

He shut off the water before helping her to her feet. Then he dried her off with one of the soft towels he'd pulled from the linen closet.

"Can you put on your clothes?" he asked.

"I've been dressing myself since I was a child," she snapped.

His lips thinned, but he didn't say anything. Instead, he pulled on his thermal underwear and turned around to catch her staring at his ass. This time he gave her a knowing smile having caught her checking him out.

Kate couldn't miss the massive cock standing out from his body in the thermals. It took all her willpower to move her eyes away from it and keep her hands from encircling it.

She quickly pulled on her pajamas. They were some of her warmest but had kittens on them. In front of Bruce, though, she felt like a kid in them. She turned her back to him and waited for him to finish getting ready.

He reached around her to open the door. Cold air rushed in, sending shivers along her skin. Bruce picked her up before she had a chance to stop him and carried her across the room in long strides to deposit her on the bed.

"Quick, get beneath the covers, Kate. You'll warm back up in no time."

"It's like a block of ice in here," she complained.

He slipped beneath the covers and pulled her over toward him. As cold as she was, she didn't protest and actually burrowed into his warmer body. He grunted when she kneed him in the stomach.

"Straighten out your legs, Kate. I'll get you warm." He reached beneath the covers, and before she realized what he had a mind to do, he'd slipped his hand into her pajama bottoms and covered her pussy with his hand.

"What are you doing?" she demanded with a yelp.

"I'm going to warm you up, Kate."

He began rubbing her pussy lips with his fingers until she parted her legs against her better judgment. It was as if her body had a mind of its own. He dipped his fingers into her already sodden pussy and rubbed them around her clit.

"Fuck, you're wet already, Kate. Are you wanting more than my fingers in your cunt, baby?"

"I–I don't know. God, I can't think when you do that." She hissed out a breath and buried her face in his chest as he continued circling her clit with his moistened fingers.

It felt so good. She didn't want him to stop what he was doing for even one minute. Why did she respond to him so easily?

When he shoved them inside of her she tightened around him and called out his name. Never had she felt anything like this. What was he doing to her? The feel of his fingers inside her body thrilled her, but also scared her. She'd never known a man to pleasure her this way. She was used to the quick clumsy attentions of the boys back home when she had been in school. This was nothing like that.

"Fuck, you're tight. Does this feel good, baby?" He began to rub a spot inside of her that curled her toes.

Kate arched her back as he stroked the sweet spot that he had found. She couldn't say anything. Her voice was locked deep within her where small electrical impulses jumped and danced along her clit. Even her nipples were peaking from the sensations Bruce was causing.

"Please," she cried out, not knowing what she was begging for.

"What do you need, Kate?" he whispered in her ear. "What do you need from me?"

"I don't know. I need more." She couldn't make up her mind. All she knew for certain was that only he could give it to her now.

He fingered her pussy then stroked her cunt until she was wild with need. Then he returned to her clit and massaged it until lightning struck her, sending shards of fire throughout her body. Her body convulsed. Bruce sought out her mouth and kissed her.

His lips smoothed over hers, and then his tongue licked along the seam of her lips until he pressed on her clit and she opened her mouth in a silent scream. He took advantage of it and stroked his tongue along hers. When he licked the roof of her mouth, she finally joined in and tangled her tongue with his.

When he pulled away and stroked her pussy until she was calm again, Kate realized she was indeed warm all over. Her face burned with shame that she'd just begged him to take her. Tears threatened to fall. She tried to turn over, but he pulled her closer to him.

"Shh, Kate. There's no need to be embarrassed. We're your men now, and we'll be pleasuring you often, baby." He brushed a tear from her eyes and pushed back a strand of hair behind her ear.

"It's not right. We aren't married, and two men can't marry one woman anyway." She refused to look him in the eye.

"Times have changed, Kate. The only way to keep a woman safe is to have two or three men to watch over her. There are vicious men out there waiting to steal a woman. You know that. Mike knew it even before this happened. I'm sorry it's like that, but it is." He seemed to hesitate then asked, "Were you already attracted to someone else?"

"No. I just didn't want my brother to give me to someone I didn't know," she admitted.

"You know us, Kate. We've been around enough lately that you should be fairly comfortable with us."

"It doesn't make it right, though." She sighed and hoped he would just go to sleep.

"I don't want you to feel forced into this, Kate. We're not barbarians or rapists."

"I know that. I can't deny that you made me feel good. Neither can I deny that I wanted you, but it feels wrong to want two men at the same time.

She hung her head. No, she couldn't deny it. He'd seduced her, but she had let him. Perhaps some part of her wanted them. But why? They were older than she was, and more knowledgeable. They were big men all over. Even now she could feel Bruce's hard cock poking at her stomach. He'd pressed it into her when she'd come earlier.

Some part of her was curious about what men like Bruce and Marcus could do to her. Bruce had just given her an orgasm unlike anything she'd ever had on her own. Would it always be like that, though? Would they normally just take what they wanted from her? She guessed time would tell, because she belonged to them now. Even if Mike lived, he had signed her over to them. As mad as she was at him for doing so without talking to her about it, she couldn't say that she was unhappy with them. Deep down, she had already chosen them but thought they were still grieving for their wife. She'd even felt guilty for thinking like that about them.

"Stop thinking it to death, Kate. Everything will be fine. Just give it time." He ran his hand up and down her back. Then he tangled his hand in her hair and drew her closer. "Now go to sleep, baby."

Kate closed her eyes and almost as if he'd ordered it, she fell asleep.

* * * *

"Bruce? Wake up. I need Kate to wake up. Mike is running a high temp and asking for her."

Bruce cursed. If they lost Mike, they might never truly have Kate. He leaned in toward her ear.

"Kate, baby. Wake up. Mike needs you." Bruce shook her slightly and she moaned.

"What? What's wrong?" She came awake then as if knowing. "It's Mike. What's wrong?" She started trying to climb over Bruce, but he held her still.

"Careful. I don't want you to break your neck falling out of bed. Mike's running a high fever. Let's get you downstairs." He threw back the cover and cursed as the cold air hit his bare chest.

Bruce knew she wouldn't wait for either of them to get dressed, so he grabbed his shirt and socks and made sure Kate did the same. Then he followed her downstairs to the living room. Mike was tossing and turning on the couch. His flushed red face registered as being hot with fever.

"Mike. Can you hear me, Mike?" Kate took her brother's hand and squeezed it.

"Kate? I'm sorry, Kate. I did what I thought was best," Mike managed to get out in a gravelly voice.

"It's okay, Mike. Just get well for me. I can't deal with it if you die on me. Please don't give up."

Bruce watched as Kate struggled not to cry over her brother. He would do anything to help the young man, but this was up to God now. They could only do so much. He wanted to hold her and take away her pain, but that was beyond his ability as well.

Kate spent the next several hours bathing Mike in cool water. She talked to him almost the entire time about their past and a future where she was with him.

Bruce joined Marcus in the kitchen and poured a cup of coffee. His brother sipped on his then shook his head as Kate hurried in to change out the water for more cold water. Bruce took the large bowl and emptied it for her then filled it and carried it back to the living room. When he got back, Marcus was shaking his head again.

"What?"

"She's desperate for him to live, Bruce. If he doesn't, and I don't see it happening, she's going to be devastated."

"He's her brother, Marcus. Of course she is."

"Yeah, but she's counting on him to keep her with him." He ran his hand up and down the mug.

"She knows that's not going to happen. But she's scared. As long as Mike is around, she thinks she is safe. I hope he lives. I would hate for her to lose her security."

"We'd never hurt her, Bruce."

"I know that and you know that, but she doesn't."

"I guess you're right," Marcus said. I want her to be happy, Bruce. I love her. I've loved her almost from the beginning."

"I know. If she loses Mike, she's not going to be happy for a long while. We'll just have to deal with it." Bruce ran a hand over his face.

"Marcus?" Kate walked in.

"What is it, baby?" He stood up and walked toward her.

"Mike is sweating now. Should I keep bathing him?"

"Let's go look." He looked over at Bruce then followed Kate back into the other room.

Bruce sighed. Maybe God was looking out for all of them after all. He stood up and walked into the living room. Marcus was checking Mike while Kate wrung her hands watching.

"He's better, right?"

"His fever is breaking. That's good, Kate. Let's keep him covered until it's down to one hundred. Then we'll dry him off and put dry clothes on him.

Nearly an hour later, he was running a low-grade fever and his color was back to a more normal pink tint. Kate cried the entire time they changed his clothes. It took all three of them to dry him off and re-dress him in thermal underwear and socks. Then they re-covered him.

"Thanks, both of you. He's going to be okay now. I just know it." Kate hugged them both then went back to tending to her brother.

"It's going to be a long healing process, Kate. He's still got quite a ways to go," Bruce warned her.

"I know, but he's going to be okay. That's all that matters." She held on to her brother's hand, using it like a lifeline. As if as long as she was touching him, she was safe.

Bruce sighed. At least she wouldn't be afraid. That was important. Then he wondered what Mike would do once he was back on his feet. Would he stick around or leave Kate with them and move off somewhere? That would hurt Kate worse than if he'd died.

Kate yawned and stretched. She had been on her feet caring for Mike for nearly six hours now and operating on less than five hours of sleep. They all three needed a nap. He knew he would never get her to leave Mike. He looked over at Marcus stretched out on the recliner.

"Kate, baby. You're tired. You need a nap."

"I'm not leaving Mike. Not until he wakes up and is coherent."

"Why don't you sleep with Marcus over there in the recliner? You'll be right here with him, and I can wake you if he wakes up."

"Oh, well. I can stretch out here on the floor. I'll be fine." She started to sit down, but Bruce caught her.

"No you don't. You're not sleeping on a cold floor. You'll sleep with Marcus. You can keep each other warm." He scooped her up and deposited her in Marcus's lap.

His brother opened an eye and wrapped his arms around her. "Hey, Kate. You feel good. Keep me warm."

Kate opened her mouth then closed it and sighed. She settled down and got comfortable. Bruce watched as she slowly fell asleep. His brother's smile told him that Marcus was happy to have her in his arms. He knew how it felt to hold her—peaceful. Bruce hoped that one day, she'd feel that same peace being in their arms.

He settled down to watch after Mike while the other slept. The man seemed to be breathing well and had kept his natural pink coloring ever since the fever had broken. He kept the fire going and waited for the three of them to wake up.

Chapter Nine

"Kate?"

Mike's voice roused Bruce from his thoughts. He leaned forward from his chair and felt the young man's forehead. It felt cool to the touch.

"Where's Kate?" Mike asked.

"She's asleep over there in the chair with Marcus. How are you feeling?"

"Tired, but okay. She's okay? They didn't hurt her?"

"She's fine, Mike. Other than being worried sick about you." Bruce stood up and stretched. "I'll wake her up so you can talk to her. It will go a long way to settling her nerves."

"Let her sleep. We need to talk." Mike coughed.

"Here, let me get you some water." Bruce hurried to the kitchen and got a fresh glass of water. He carried it back to Mike and helped the man sit up enough to drink from the glass.

"What did you want to talk about, Mike?" Bruce was scared he was going to want to take Kate back.

"I had papers written up on Kate so I could find her a couple of good men to take care of her. I know you're still grieving over your late wife, but I want you to take Kate. I think you'll make her happy and take good care of her."

"You told us all of this when we were about to take the bullet out. I have the papers in my wallet." Bruce watched Mike's face. A look of relief washed over it.

"So you'll take her?" Mike asked.

"I guess we've already done that since I have the papers and she was there when you told us." Bruce looked over to where she still lay sleeping in Marcus's arms. "She's not happy about it at all, Mike. You need to settle her some."

"I expect I'll need to do that. I guess there were extenuating circumstances the other day."

"I guess there were." Bruce drew in a deep breath and asked the question that was worrying him. "What are your plans now that you've found Kate a home?"

"I was planning on sticking around at the house where we are living now, but if you think that will just make it harder on her settling down, I can move on." Mike didn't look like he liked that idea much.

"I think that if you dump her on us and then leave, she'll never forgive any of us."

"She may never forgive me anyway," Mike said with a pained smile.

"You're right. I probably never will." Kate crawled out of Marcus's lap.

Marcus grunted when she elbowed him in the gut. He righted the recliner to help her get out.

"How are you feeling?" she asked her brother.

"I feel pretty good for someone who got shot." He grinned then sobered up at her frown. "Seriously, I'm fine, Kate. What about you? Did they hurt you?"

"No. Just some bruises, is all." She knelt beside him. "I was so scared I had lost you, Mike."

"Well, you didn't. I'm right here. I'll be back up in no time."

"Why did you do it, Mike?" she asked in a soft voice.

"Because you need someone who can keep you safe and make you happy. I couldn't keep you safe. That's pretty damn obvious now, I would think."

"You signed me over to them without even consulting me."

"I was going to talk to you about it as soon as we got everything taken care of in the garden. You were relaxed around them, more so than anyone else. I thought you would be happier with Bruce and Marcus then anyone else."

"But you got papers made on me and *gave* me to them. Like a gift or something." She shook her head. "I'm not something to just give away, Mike. Besides being a human being, I'm your sister."

"It's done, Kate. You belong to them now. I'm sorry, but it's the only way to keep you safe. Please be happy. Give them a chance to show you that they can make you that way." Mike was pleading with her.

Bruce felt for the other man. He was doing what he thought was best for his sister. Kate, however, saw it as a betrayal of sorts. Maybe he could see it both ways. He stood up and went to Kate.

"Let's see about making something he can eat. He needs to eat to get strong." Kate readily went with him to the kitchen.

"I'll fix him some broth from the deer meat Marcus brought in. But it doesn't change the fact that he's basically just giving me away."

"Wouldn't your father be giving you away if you were getting married?" Bruce asked.

"That's different. I would have chosen my husband myself, and it would only have been one husband, not two." She talked while she cut up meat for the broth.

"Which of us would you have picked if you had to pick one of us?" he asked.

"I–I don't know." She faltered in her movements then shrugged. "It really doesn't matter, though, since I am stuck with both of you, and I don't have a say in it."

"I want you to be content here, Kate. Marcus and I will do everything we can to make you happy, but you have to decide that you want to be before it will happen."

Kate didn't look back at him as she set about making the broth. "I need some time, Bruce. This isn't what I wanted out of life. It wasn't what I had hoped for."

"I would guess we have all the time in the world, Kate. Just don't take too long." Bruce left her in the kitchen and returned to the living room where Marcus and Mike were talking.

* * * *

Kate felt the tears slide down her face as she stirred the broth for Mike. She was forever grateful that Mike was going to be okay, but she was furious with him at the same time for what he had done. She cut up more of the deer steak and made gravy to go over it then sat it in the oven to simmer until she had finished feeding Mike.

When she walked in the room thirty minutes later, it was to find that Mike had fallen asleep. She gently woke him up and helped him eat the broth then left him to rest while she fixed their meal.

Her mind circled around and around as she cooked. She was attracted to both men, and of the available ones she had met, they would have been her first choice, but it was the principle of the matter. He had made the decision for her. They said they would never hurt her, but she really didn't know them well enough to believe them. Neither did Mike, for that matter. Sure, he'd spent more time with them than she had, but it had been all of about six or maybe seven months.

With a heavy sigh, Kate called the men in to eat. She filled their plates from the stove and waited for them to dig in before she fixed her plate. Bruce just looked at her.

"What?" she asked. "Did I forget something?" She looked around the kitchen.

"Where is your plate?" he asked.

"I was waiting to see if you needed anything else before I sat down."

"Fix your plate, Kate, and come sit with us," Marcus said.

She added deer meat with gravy and beans to her plate then sat down at the head of the table. It was all that was open. Once she sat down, the men began to eat. Kate picked at her food, not really hungry. She had too much on her mind to stomach much.

"This is good, Kate. Why aren't you eating yours?" Bruce asked.

"I'm not really hungry. I nibbled while I was cooking it."

"Eat a bit more, Kate. I don't want you falling sick from malnourishment."

Marcus rose from his seat and took his plate over to the sink. Bruce waited on her to finish eating before he got up. She hurriedly took another bite of her deer meat and swallowed it down so he would be happy.

"That's all I can eat. I'm really not hungry."

Bruce merely nodded and took her plate with his. He and Marcus did the dishes while she watched. She got up and tended to the leftovers then walked back into the living room to check on Mike. He was still sound asleep. She wandered over to the windows and looked outside. To her surprise, it was snowing. She hurried back into the kitchen.

"It's snowing. Did you know?" She couldn't keep the grin from her face.

"I knew it was probably going to, but I didn't realize it had started. I need to go check on the animals." Bruce handed her the drying cloth and walked over to put on his boots and coat.

"Be careful out there, Bruce. It's really coming down," Marcus said, looking out the window.

"I shouldn't be longer than an hour." He opened the back door and hurried through it to keep from letting in too much cold air.

"Do you have any animals other than cows and chickens?"

"We have some cattle and horses. They all have to be taken care of and especially in the winter time." Marcus handed her a plate to dry. "Can you milk a cow?"

"You're kidding, right? I've never even been close to a cow."

"I'll teach you how. Then you can handle the milking and gathering the eggs. That would take a lot off of us."

She frowned but nodded. For a minute she had forgotten that she belonged to them now. *Damn Mike and his arrogance.* Never mind that he thought he was doing what was best. She put away the dishes and hung the drying cloth up to dry. Then she wandered back into the living room. Mike was awake again. He smiled at her despite the fact that she frowned at him.

"I love you, Kate. You know that, right?" he asked.

"I love you, too, Mike. Doesn't change the fact that you gave me to two strangers."

"Damn it, Kate. They aren't strangers. We've known them for over half a year now and had them over to eat at the house." Mike was angry now.

Kate didn't much care if he was. She was hurt, and still a tiny bit uncertain. Was he going to leave her once he got well? Would he go off to find himself a woman and forget about her? What would be the difference in keeping his wife safe and keeping her safe? She almost asked him that, but Marcus walked in, and she decided against it.

The three of them talked about the weather, the animals, and things in general while they waited on Bruce to come back in. When an hour passed, Kate began to worry.

"Do you think you should go out and check on him?" she asked Marcus.

"He's fine. It takes time to tend to all of them, and in the snow, it takes longer. He'll be in before long." Marcus didn't seem worried so Kate tried to curb hers as well.

Sure enough, twenty minutes later, Bruce walked through the kitchen door, cursing the cold and stomping his feet to rid them of snow. Kate hurried to clean up the melting snow from the floor.

"How is everything out there?" Marcus called from the living room.

Bruce finished pulling off his coat before he answered. "Everything's fine. The cattle had wandered farther out than I expected. Had to round them up closer to the house. Chickens were already in the coop, and the cow was hungry." He walked into the living room and backed up to the fireplace.

"Do you think we'll get much snow?" Mike asked him.

"Doubt it this time. I figure we've got another couple of weeks before anything big will hit. The cattle would have nosed together had it felt like much to them. I think we'll get another two or three inches before it quits. Going to be cold, though."

"Are you warm enough, Mike?" Kate asked.

"I'm toasty warm." He grinned up at her.

"Expect we better head to bed and get some rest, then. Going to need to work with the cattle tomorrow to keep them close," Bruce said. "You ready, Kate?"

"I was going to sleep down here with Mike. He might need something in the night." She squeezed her hands together in hopes they would let her.

"I don't need anything, Kate. You go on with them where you'll be in a comfortable bed. I'm fine down here."

"Mike…"

"Kate, I'm fine. Go on upstairs with them."

His no-nonsense voice always irritated her. She huffed out a breath and turned and walked up the stairs without saying good night. She hoped he didn't need anything, but if he did, it served him right.

When Bruce's hands began to pull off her sweatshirt, she stilled. He pulled it over her head then worked on pulling off her thermal top as well. Marcus unfastened her jeans and pulled them down until she stepped out of them. Having one man undress her was sexy, but having two was downright erotic. She pulled on her nightclothes and waited to see what Bruce would do.

"Marcus. Get her warm in the bed. I'm going to take a shower. I smell like cows." Bruce disappeared into the bathroom.

"Come on, Kate. I don't want you to catch pneumonia standing out in the cold." He urged her toward the bed.

Kate climbed between the sheets and shivered while she waited on Marcus to change clothes. He pulled a pair of thermal bottoms from the dresser and climbed into them. Then he got in bed and pulled her up next to him.

"Let's get you warmed up, Kate." He rubbed up and down her arms then moved his hands lower.

Kate closed her eyes when he rubbed her mound through her pajama bottoms.

Chapter Ten

Marcus rubbed her pussy through her pajama bottoms. He could tell as soon as she began to get wet. He grinned and slipped his hand inside her bottoms to reach her now-drenched pussy. He swirled his fingers in her juices, then searched for her slit between her pussy lips. When he entered her cunt with his fingers, she moaned and tilted her pelvis toward him.

He searched out her hidden G-spot and stroked it several times when he located it. She grabbed his shoulders and pumped her hips as if she couldn't help it, and perhaps she couldn't. He located her clit and began to thumb it as he stroked her hot spot. She groaned and then bit her fist as she came unglued around him.

"Don't bite yourself, baby. If you need to bite anyone, bite me." Bruce climbed into the bed. "Marcus, she needs some loving." Bruce leaned down and kissed her.

Marcus wanted her something fierce, but wasn't sure she was ready for them. He slipped deeper under the covers and pulled her pajama bottoms down her legs and off her feet. Then he squeezed between her legs and nosed his way between her pussy lips. She shivered around him.

He licked and sucked on her pussy lips until she was moving against him once again. Then he entered her hot, wet cunt with two fingers and pumped them in and out as he licked around her clit. She moaned above him. He could just imagine Bruce sucking and licking her tits. Marcus wanted to taste the round berries for himself.

He stroked his tongue deeper into her cunt alongside his fingers in an effort to gather more of her sweet nectar. She tasted like hot candy, sweet and sticky on his tongue. Bruce would go crazy when he tasted her.

"Marcus. She's thrashing around up here. I think you need to fuck her before she goes crazy."

"God, Bruce. She tastes amazing. I don't want to stop."

"Let me taste."

Bruce pushed back the covers and slipped his fingers into her tight cunt. When he withdrew them, they were coated in her honey. He sucked them into his mouth and closed his eyes. His hum of approval seemed to ramp Kate's pleasure higher. She groaned and beat at the bed with her fists.

"Please. Do something. I'm so close. God, I'm burning alive." Her voice came out as a whimper.

"Fuck her, Marcus. I want to see her face when she comes." Bruce bent over her and took her mouth in a kiss.

Marcus positioned his cock at her slit and lifted her hips beneath his hands so he could guide his dick into her deep cunt. When he began to push his way inside, she hissed out a breath. He stilled, then pushed again as she slowly opened her body to him.

"Fuck! She's so damn tight. I'm never going to last." He pressed forward again.

"Please, Marcus. I need you." Kate's strained voice stirred something inside of him.

He pulled out and thrust forward with more power this time. Her hot cunt parted just enough that he was able to make it halfway inside of her. He pulled back and tunneled inside of her again. This time he reached the back of her womb, bumping her cervix.

"Yes!" she hissed out.

Bruce looked down at Marcus and grinned. "I think she likes it a little harder than usual, Marcus."

Marcus knew Bruce was thrilled to find that out. He enjoyed being able to let go and pummel a woman's pussy with his cock. Bruce wasn't known for being an easy lover. It was why Marcus was going first with Kate. Introducing her to love between two men would be a lesson in patience for both of them, but especially for Bruce.

Kate reached for him when he pulled back. She tried to wrap her legs around him, but with his hands holding her ass, she couldn't get them around him. She pleaded with him using her eyes.

Marcus shoved forward over and over again. Soon he was plunging his dick deeper and deeper into her cunt with every shove. She was screaming out her needs as he pummeled her pussy with his cock. When she began tightening her cunt around his dick, he groaned.

"Fuck yeah, Kate. Just like that." He concentrated on holding off his orgasm even as she squeezed him over and over.

"Damn, ah, fuck, Kate. Do that again. Yeah, just like that." He wasn't going to make it. His balls were boiling with his cum. Sparks flew down his spine as his cock bumped against her cervix.

She arched her back and screamed, going wild around him. Bruce was hanging onto her breasts with his mouth and fingers as she bucked and called out Marcus's name. He let go and shot cum deep into her sweet cunt. His balls exploded as his cock spasmed. He threw back his head and shouted her name.

He collapsed on her, barely managing to keep the major portion of his weight off of her. Bruce grinned at him.

"Move over, old man. It's my turn."

"Man you'll think old"—*pant, pant*—"when you get inside of her."

He continued to pant, trying to catch his breath. He couldn't ever remember coming that hard before. She'd squeezed it out of him. Bruce would go wild with her around his dick. He wanted to watch, but first, he had to relearn how to breathe. He collapsed on the bed again.

* * * *

Bruce doubted anyone could make him lose control as Marcus had just done. The man was strong, but not like he was. He kissed and licked the sweat from Kate's bare tummy. It quivered beneath his mouth.

"Turn over, Kate."

"Over? Why?" She looked at him with a question in her eyes.

"I want to fuck you like that. Turn over." He helped her rotate to her belly.

She rose up on all fours and looked over her shoulder at him. He could have sworn he saw a challenge there. Maybe it was just his imagination. He smoothed his hands over the silken globes of her ass. They were a pale pink. He would love to see them cherry red and warm to his touch. *Maybe another time.*

He spread her wide and entered her slickened pussy with his steel-hard cock. He was a bit longer than Marcus, whereas Marcus was thicker in girth. Bruce tunneled deep into her cunt and stopped just short of her cervix. He wanted her needy and begging for more before he bumped her there. She liked it, and it would probably send her over for him to do it if he played his cards right.

He moved slow and steady until she was complaining in frustration.

"Faster, Bruce. Go faster." She tried to take over the rhythm by thrusting back against him.

He chuckled and thrust forward against her. She moaned and hissed out a *yes* in reaction. Bruce wasn't going to let her have her way so soon. He alternated between going slow and steady to faster and harder. Soon, she was thrusting back against him harder and faster as he tunneled his way through her thick pussy juices.

When she squeezed around him the first time, it was like thrusting his cock through a tight fist. Fuck, she was hot! She was burning him alive. He concentrated on giving her pleasure. He wanted her to come harder than she ever had and to want more and more of them. He needed her to want them as much as they wanted her.

She began to chant *more, more* over and over again. He took that as the sign that she was ready for him to let go and push her limits. He dragged his thumb through her juices, and as he shoved his dick inside of her, he pushed his thumb in her back hole. She almost went still, but he bumped hard against her cervix, causing her to scream out. She went wild around him as he fucked her with his cock and his thumb over and over. The more he touched her cervix, the more she thrashed her body against his.

She clamped down on his dick like a vise.

"Fuck! Your cunt is like a hot fist milking my cock, Kate." He grabbed her hip with one hand and began pummeling her in an effort to drive her over the edge before he could no longer hold back his own climax.

"That's it, baby. Oh, fuck! More, Kate. More." He wanted it all. He wanted all she could give.

When she finally exploded around his cock, her quivering cunt milked at his dick in long, tight squeezes until he felt his balls draw even tighter, and he shot cum deep inside of her. His ass cheeks squeezed tight as he felt his toes curling. He couldn't stop thrusting through her tight cunt, though. Not until she relaxed and whimpered at his assault. Then he stopped and licked a line up her back to her neck. He sought out the soft skin of her shoulder and bit down and sucked until he was sure he'd left a mark.

Kate collapsed beneath him. He gently pulled out then nodded at Marcus while he headed for the bathroom. Marcus would cuddle with her while he cleaned up and prepared a warm, wet cloth to clean her up. She wouldn't sleep well wet and sticky.

When he returned, she was laying half on Marcus and half off, her head over his chest. Bruce smiled and began cleaning her up. She whimpered and protested, but Marcus soothed her and she calmed down.

Once he had discarded the cloth, he climbed into bed beneath the covers to cuddle up against her back. She actually pushed her ass against his groin and left it there. Maybe she would adjust easier than he had worried about. He sure hoped so. Then she stiffened all over.

"What's wrong, Kate?" Marcus asked her.

"He heard me, didn't he?" She buried her face against Marcus's chest.

"Mike?" Bruce asked.

"Yes," she whispered.

"He knows we're going to take care of you, baby," Bruce told her.

"But I screamed."

"He'll just know we took very good care of you," Marcus teased her.

Bruce wasn't so sure it was a good idea to tease her. She didn't appear to appreciate it.

"I can't believe I let you do that to me with him here." She began to struggle to get away from them.

"Easy, Kate. Slow down. We're your husbands now. You're our wife. Sex is natural between us. Don't act like it's not." Bruce wrapped an arm around her waist.

"I'm so embarrassed. My brother shouldn't hear me do that. It's not right." There were tears in her voice.

Bruce and Marcus looked at each other. Had they made a tactical error in judgment? Maybe having her scream out her orgasms hadn't been a good idea with Mike downstairs. Lord knew if it were his sister, it would piss him off knowing someone was having sex with her. He didn't think it mattered that Mike was two years younger than Kate.

"Go to sleep, Kate. We'll work it all out in the morning. You need rest and to sleep. Mike's doing great and will be well before you know it."

"You didn't even want another wife," Kate whispered as she fell asleep.

Bruce stiffened then relaxed. No, he hadn't wanted another one. Marcus had, though, so they could make this work. Marcus would give her all the love and attention she needed, and he would help keep her safe and make sure she was satisfied in bed. He didn't have to love her to help keep her happy. After several minutes of trying to force himself to relax, Bruce finally drifted off to sleep with the thought of losing Kate uppermost in his head.

* * * *

Kate woke early the next morning to find herself sandwiched between the two men. She was almost on top of Marcus, with Bruce curled around her back. She was toasty warm and rested, but immediately uneasy. How could she face Mike after the noises she had made last night? She would never be able to look him in the eyes again without blushing.

"What is it, Kate?" Bruce kissed her shoulder and pulled back from her.

She rolled off of Marcus, causing him to grunt and pull the covers tighter around him.

"How am I supposed to face my brother again after last night?" She couldn't hide the tears in her voice.

"Baby, he knew when we walked up those stairs what was going to happen. He wouldn't have let you go if he hadn't approved. He did choose us as your husbands."

She swallowed and started to climb down the middle of the bed. Bruce grabbed her around the waist and pulled her back against him.

"Where are you going, Katie girl?" He wrapped his legs around one of hers.

She could feel his hardened cock against her ass cheeks. Surely he didn't want sex now. When he reached between her legs and fingered her pussy, she realized he did. He expertly manipulated her pussy and clit until she was weeping between her legs for him. He entered her with two fingers and began to slowly fuck her in and out with them. Kate wanted to tell him no, but couldn't. She wanted him now with a vengeance. All it had taken was for him to finger her clit and she was on the verge of coming.

He rolled over on top of her and took her mouth with his. The kiss was wild, untamed, and titillating. He thrust his tongue into her mouth and twined it with hers before exploring her mouth with it. He teased and tempted until she was giving hers to him to suck and nip. The kiss seemed to go on forever. She might have missed his slipping inside of her if he hadn't pulled back and cursed.

"Fuck, you're tight, baby. Your cunt feels like a hot, wet fist squeezing my dick."

After a couple of false starts, he pushed until he was all the way inside of her. God, it felt good to have him inside her like that. He filled her up and even touched a part of her she hadn't realized needed touching. He almost managed it, but she needed more. More of what, she didn't know.

He thrust his cock deeper and deeper until he was bumping her cervix with each thrust. Her clit brushed against the hair of his groin with each pump of his dick inside her pussy. She felt the beginnings of something hot and heavy building in her clit from her spine. He stared down at her with his dark, brooding eyes.

"Play with your tits for me, baby. I want to see you pinch those sweet berries for me."

"I–I can't touch myself like that." She was horrified.

"You touch yourself when you're alone, don't you?"

"But not when someone is watching," she whispered.

He had stopped fucking her now and was watching her.

"Touch yourself, Kate. I need to see you pleasure yourself."

"But…" She couldn't think as he flexed inside of her.

"Do it, baby. You can do it. I know you can." He took one of her hands and placed it over her breast.

She shuddered, but raised her other hand to the opposite breast. Then she squeezed them softly at first. She slowly began to pull on the nipples. She had her eyes squeezed shut as she pretended no one was there but her.

Bruce shattered that pretense, though, when he pulled out and shoved his cock all the way inside of her, bumping her cervix with enough force to draw a gasp from her. She squeezed her nipples tighter and pulled on them. Her eyes flew open when he nipped at her chin.

"Watch us, baby. Watch as my cock buries itself inside your hot cunt. God, I love seeing that. I want to feel you squeeze me tight when you come, baby. Make yourself come for me."

Kate opened her mouth to deny that she could, but already, the combination of her fingers at her breasts and his cock pumping into her pussy was bringing her to the edge. Electricity shot from her nipples to her clit and back again. Heat burned inside of her. When he reached down and pinched her clit, she buried her hand in her mouth to keep from screaming. He tunneled in and out of her wet pussy then covered her and pulled her hand from her mouth.

"Bite me, Kate. Sink those little teeth into me."

Kate latched on to his shoulder and bit. He growled but didn't stop her. She sucked instead of screamed now as her climax slowly wound down. He didn't pull away from her, but instead, he let her let go on her own.

"Mike never heard a thing, Kate. You don't have to worry about it again. We'll help you keep quiet."

Kate looked at his shoulder and felt equal parts pleasure and shame warring inside of her. The fact that she had marked him as he had marked her gave her a certain amount of pride. The fact that he had let her do it told her that he at least cared about how she felt. It also told her that he had no intentions of not having sex to appease her sense of propriety with her brother downstairs.

She swallowed hard around the knot blocking her throat and quietly crawled from the bed. She quickly closed herself in the bathroom and got ready for the day. How was she going to reconcile her heart and her mind to live with these two men? She knew they hadn't wanted another wife, much less her. Mike had forced her on them and expected them to be fine with it. How could he have done this to all three of them?

A knock at the door stilled her hand as she ran the brush through her hair.

"Kate? Can I come in?" Marcus's voice reached her from the other side of the door.

"Come in, Marcus."

"You okay, baby?"

"Yeah, just dandy." She sighed and turned to leave.

Marcus pulled her into his arms and kissed her before he let her go. He looked into her eyes and smiled down at her.

"Dress warm, baby. I'm going to show you the animals this morning before we have to go see about the cattle."

"Okay." She smiled back. She would let him show her and pretend that everything was normal when in fact, there was nothing normal about anything in the world anymore.

Chapter Eleven

Kate finished cleaning up the breakfast dishes as the men discussed what their plans were for the day. Mike was dozing again after having eaten a fairly good plateful. His color was better, and he didn't act as if he'd heard a thing the night before. Either he had been sound asleep or he was a great actor. Kate figured he had been asleep. He had never been able to lie very well.

"You about ready, Kate?" Marcus asked.

"Yes, I just need to get my coat and gloves on." She pulled on her coat and searched in her pocket for gloves.

"Where are you taking her?" Bruce asked.

"I thought I would introduce her to the animals while I get the milk and the eggs this morning." Marcus wound a scarf he'd gotten from somewhere around her neck.

"You do exactly like Marcus tells you. There are dangerous wolves out there. Don't leave his sight for any reason at all." Bruce was holding her upper arms in his hands.

"I'll be careful, Bruce." She tugged at her arms.

He seemed to realize he was holding her and released her after rubbing his hands up and down her arms. Then he donned his own coat and walked out the kitchen door.

"He's worried about you, baby. Just stay with me and everything will be fine."

Marcus took one of her gloved hands and led her through the kitchen doorway and out into the swirling snow. He grabbed a shovel and shoveled a path for them after handing her the egg basket and milk pail. When they reached the chicken coop, he had her stand back while he opened the door. Nothing happened. He grinned and nodded for her to follow him inside.

The hens were all clucking and sitting on their nests. When Marcus slipped his hands beneath them and pulled out their eggs, they squawked but didn't put up a fight.

"Your turn."

Kate tried to mimic his method but got pecked for her effort. She managed to grab one egg out of three tries.

"What am I doing wrong?" she said after a particularly vicious attack by one hen.

"One thing is you have to be confident. The other thing is don't ruffle their feathers when you pull out the egg." He grinned. "It takes time. In the summertime, I still end up with peck marks on my hands and wrists."

"Well, don't expect me to get the hang of it too quickly. I don't like to be pecked with gloves on, much less without."

Marcus laughed and finished gathering the eggs. Again he had Kate wait behind him while he opened the coop door and stepped out. When nothing happened, he held out his hand for her to follow him. This time, he led her to what looked like a barn. Inside, it was a little warmer than outside since there was no wind and there were several animals in the barn to keep the heat up some.

"Why were you so careful around the chicken coop?" she asked.

"A woman was attacked last year while she was gathering eggs. Wolves love chickens, so we have to be careful around them to be sure they aren't waiting around."

"Oh." She shivered at the thought of wolves waiting for her to come out and get eggs.

"Okay, here is Sunshine." He indicated at large cow chewing on some hay.

"Hi, Sunshine." She shrugged. "Does she know her name?"

"Yeah, but she doesn't know you yet, so she's ignoring you. Right, girl?"

The cow turned her head and swished her tail.

"Now watch what I do." He placed the pail beneath the cow's udder and using two fingers from each hand began pulling on the cow's teats. Milk began to spray into the bucket. "It's all in how you squeeze, and the rhythm. Now you try." He started to get up.

"Oh no. Not this time. I'll try next time. I want to watch you and let Elsie here…"

"Sunshine."

"Sunshine get used to me." She walked over to where the cow was chomping on hay and reached out and patted the cow's head. The heifer just chewed and ignored her.

Kate walked back to where Marcus was steadily filling the bucket and watched how his hands worked. They were strong hands, but they were so gentle on the cow. They had been gentle with her the night before. She drew in a deep breath and tried to put the night before out of her mind. It wasn't easy after Bruce had taken her that morning. Still, she had so much more to think about other than sex. It might be a big part of their lives, but it wasn't the most important part. At least it shouldn't be.

"What are you thinking so hard about there, Katie girl?"

"Nothing really. Just wondering what it's going to be like this winter. I've never lived anywhere that got so much snow. You've been here for what, six years now? Tell me about what you do in the winter." Kate couldn't imagine staying inside the entire time.

"Winters are hard here, Kate. It snows in feet here, not in inches. We have to keep the path to the chickens and the barn shoveled. We also have to keep the one out to the fence line so we can keep hay thrown over the fence for the cattle to eat." He continued milking the cow in the strangely hypnotic rhythm.

"Staying warm is the hardest thing during that time. You'll help by keeping wood in the fireplace for us so that we can warm up between trips outside."

"I can do that. I've kept a fireplace before. We had one at home. Too bad you don't have gas logs, though. That would mean less work for you chopping wood."

"Bruce has been talking about maybe running a pipe and putting a gas stove in. We don't want to mess up the fireplace in case we ever have to do without gas. Right now we trade a cow a year for the use of the gas, but that could change."

"I can't imagine how we would survive without gas. How would we cook?"

"We'd manage, Kate. Don't worry about it right now. We have gas for the stove, so you don't need to worry about it." Marcus stood up and picked up the bucket of milk.

"Think you can do it tomorrow?" he asked.

"You're kidding, right? I don't think I can ever do it." She frowned. "Am I really supposed to be able to do it after one day?"

Marcus chuckled. "No, Kate. It will take some practice, but that means you have to actually *try* to milk the cow next time."

"I will. Just don't expect much."

"Grab the eggs, and let's get you back to the house so I can help Bruce with the cattle."

"Can I make a snowman? Marcus?"

"Not without one of us with you. I'm serious about the wolves, baby. You can't mess around with them." Marcus opened the door to the kitchen and they bustled inside out of the cold. They pulled off their boots to keep from tracking in the snow.

"Kate! Is that you?" Mike's voice carried from the living room.

"Is something wrong, Mike?" She sat the eggs on the counter and hurried to the living room.

"No, I just didn't know who it was. I'm ready to get off this couch. Think I could sit up in the kitchen with you for a while?"

Marcus walked in. "I don't see why not. You're doing pretty well. I'll help you in there."

Kate smiled at her brother. "Great. You can keep me company while I cook." She stood aside as Marcus helped Mike walk into the kitchen and settle into one of the kitchen chairs at the table.

"How do you feel now?" Marcus asked.

"Much better, thanks."

"I'm going to go now, Kate. We'll be in around noon for an hour or two then go back out after that." Marcus stepped back into his boots and kissed her on the cheek before hurrying back out the door.

"Let me get a blanket to go around you. You'll get sick again if you don't stay warm." She hurried back to the living room and grabbed his blanket. Then she wrapped it around him and looped it under his socked feet to keep them off the cold floor.

"Thanks, sis."

"You haven't called me that since third grade."

"Do you miss Mom and Dad?"

"Of course I do. Every day."

"I worry sometimes that I'm not handling things like I should be."

"You're doing the best you can, Mike. I know I've given you a hard time, but I still love you."

"They didn't hurt you, did they?"

Kate felt heat pour up her neck and cheeks. He had heard and no doubt felt helpless to do anything about it. For his sake, she would have to pretend that she was completely happy. Maybe in time she would be, but right now, she needed him to believe she was.

"No, Mike. They didn't hurt me."

He sighed and turned his head to look out the window. Kate recognized that he wouldn't bring it up again. She would have to if she wanted to talk about it, something she never would do with her brother. It wasn't something you talked about between brothers and sisters.

"I'm thinking chili tonight. What do you think, Mike?" She busied herself at the sink.

"That sounds great. What are you going to fix them for lunch?"

"I was thinking about making a shepherd's pie. It will fill them up, and there will be plenty for all of us for one meal."

Mike kept a constant chatter with her as she set about making the pie. She used potatoes, carrots, and deer meat for the insides and mixed up a pie crust for the outside. She was just pulling it out of the oven when the men walked inside bringing a swirl of snow and cold air with them.

"Pull off your boots at the door," she reminded them.

They dutifully removed their boots as they pulled off their coats, hats, and gloves. Bruce nodded at Mike and walked over to wash up in the sink.

"Use the washroom sink. I just cleaned that one up from the last time you used it." Bruce frowned but did as she asked. Marcus followed behind him.

"Kate, maybe you shouldn't fuss at them in their house," Mike suggested.

"Either I'm their wife or not, Mike. If I am, then the kitchen is my domain and I want it kept clean."

"I heard that, Katie girl," Bruce said.

"Good. Don't forget it." She smiled and carried the dish over to the table where she had already set the table for their lunch.

"Smells good," Marcus said.

Bruce walked over and took a seat next to Mike. "How are you feeling?"

"Much better now that I'm sitting up. I was beginning to get sore from lying on the couch so long. I want to walk around some tomorrow."

"Don't push it, man. You're welcome here as long as it takes. You won't have Kate at home to help you once you go back."

Kate hugged Mike lightly. "Are you already tired of me?"

Mike leaned his head back against her waist. "No. I just figure you'll do better once I'm out of your hair."

"No I won't. I don't want you to go, Mike." She felt something inside of her tearing.

"No one's going anywhere yet," Marcus said as they all sat down to eat. "This smells delicious."

The three men managed to eat every crumb of the meal and still have room for dessert. She pulled out one of the apple pies she had made and divided it up three ways. Once she had served it, Bruce grabbed her by the wrist and pulled her over to him.

"Where's yours?"

"I didn't want any, or I would have divided in four pieces."

"You hardly ate anything at lunch. You need to eat, Kate, to keep up your strength. Winters are hard here." Bruce looked almost angry to her.

"I know. Marcus told me. Ask Mike. I don't eat a lot."

"She's telling the truth, Bruce. She never has been much of an eater."

"Sit in my lap, Kate." Bruce pulled her down until she was sitting there.

He forked up a piece of the pie and held it in front of her mouth.

"Just one bite for me, Kate. That's all."

"Why?"

"I want to feed you, baby. Eat one bite just for me."

Kate looked into his eyes and saw something there that had her opening her mouth for him. He fed her the small piece of pie then took a bite himself. She sat there until he had finished his. Then she stood up and took everyone's plates. What had happened just then? She couldn't fathom what was going through Bruce's head.

While she washed dishes, the men gathered in the living room again. She had no idea what they were talking about, but she had things on her mind as well. Most of her things were still at the other house, and Mike was planning to go back there to live. How would she feel once she was alone with the two men she now belonged to?

She was fairly sure they wouldn't hurt her. They seemed like nice men all in all, but Kate still wasn't sure about being theirs to do with as they wished. Just because they were good men and wouldn't hurt her didn't mean they wouldn't want things from her she couldn't give. Like instant obedience. She had never been one to blindly obey. And then there was love.

Kate couldn't see them falling in love with her. Well, Marcus maybe, but not Bruce. He seemed to only tolerate her at times. Then, she guessed she couldn't blame him. He had been saddled with her when he was obviously still in love with his dead wife. She felt for him. She missed her parents something awful, especially her mom. What was two years when Bruce and Marcus had loved her? It had been six for her.

She finished up the dishes and walked over to the kitchen door to look out the window. She could still see the tracks from where the men had come inside earlier. The snow seemed to be slowing down like Bruce had predicted. He had said another couple of weeks before the real stuff began to fall.

"What are you thinking about, Katie girl?" Marcus pressed his body against the back of hers.

"About the snow. When this clears up we need to go back to my house, I mean Mike's house, and get my clothes before the real snow starts."

"Good idea. We'll do that." He kissed the side of her neck. "We're about to go back out now. Do you need anything before we go?"

"No, thanks. I'm going to do some cleaning."

"I've got a better idea." Bruce walked in.

Kate turned around in Marcus's arms.

"Why don't you move all of our clothes out of our old rooms into the master bedroom? Be sure and leave yourself plenty of space for your things."

"Oh, um, okay. I can do that."

"Okay, baby. We better get back out there. We'll be in before dark." Marcus kissed her then walked off to put on his boots, coat, hat, and gloves.

Bruce finished buttoning up his coat and settled his hat on his head. He bent down and kissed her on the cheek before opening the door and walking outside. Marcus followed close behind.

She cleaned up the smattering of snow on the floor and set about starting dinner. The chili would simmer all afternoon and be ready that night when they came back. She could work on the bedrooms while it cooked.

"Mike?" She walked into the living room to find him fast asleep. She sighed. *So much for company while I cook.*

Kate made the chili with beef from one of what she assumed was their cows. Once she had it simmering on the back burner, she left it to get to work on the men's clothes. She tiptoed up the stairs to keep from waking Mike.

The first room she entered happened to be Marcus's. She could tell by the haphazard way he kept his clothes. He wasn't a slouch or a slob by any means, but he didn't bother keeping his clothes neat in the drawers. She carried them into the master bedroom and put them up. Once she had all of his clothes put away, she gathered up his bathroom items and set them up in the master bathroom as well. It looked like he and Bruce were using the same bathroom anyway. She stripped Marcus's bed and piled the sheets in the hall to wash later.

Next, she walked into Bruce's room. It was immaculate for a man's room. The clothes were all put up and in neat stacks in the drawers. His bed was even neatly made. Kate transferred his clothes to the other room. She emptied his closet and lined them on the opposite side of the one in the master bedroom from his brother's clothes. When she got on a stool to check the shelves above in his old one, she found a small stack of women's clothes. She held one up and found it was made for a much thinner woman. It had to be their first wife's clothes. She folded it up and replaced it where she found it.

Finding that hidden stack proved to her that Bruce wasn't over Irene. She had heard them use her name several times when they had been at the house. Irene was obviously much smaller than she was. She would never be a tiny thing with her big bones and wide hips. She sighed. Yet another reason she wasn't the woman for them. Mike had really screwed this up. But she would make the best of it.

If nothing else, Mike having nearly died because of her made her realize that it wasn't fair to him to continue to hold onto him. It was keeping him from finding his own wife and having a life outside of her. If Marcus and Bruce could deal with her being there, then she could, too.

Chapter Twelve

Bruce stared at the stool in the closet of his old bedroom. She'd found Irene's clothes. What had she done with them? He reached up and found they were still there. Everything else in the room had been cleared out, but she had left Irene's clothes on the shelf like she had found them. He hung his head and cursed whatever had possessed him to have her move their things. He had wanted to drive home the fact that they were going to be living together and sleeping together from then on.

That he had actually forgotten about Irene's things being up in his closet surprised him. He had often taken them down and held them to his face in an effort to remember her scent. He missed her and felt like it was his fault she had died like she had. He didn't think Marcus even knew that he had some of her things in his room.

Would Kate say anything or just pretend she hadn't found them? He wouldn't blame her for saying something. She was their wife now. Something inside of him told him to get rid of Irene's things, but he didn't do it. He would leave them where they were for now.

He walked out of the bedroom straight into Kate. She turned haunted eyes up to him.

"Sorry. I was just coming to tell you that dinner is on the table." She turned and walked away.

She knew he had come to check to see if she'd done anything with the other woman's clothes. *Fuck!* Bruce ran a hand over his face and followed her down the stairs.

Marcus and Mike were already at the table eating. Kate spooned chili into her bowl and sat down. Her place was at the head of the table with Mike at the opposite end. He and Marcus sat on either side of the table.

Mike and Marcus kept up a general conversation around the table which he joined in. Kate didn't. She ate her chili and spooned out second helpings to the men. Then she got up and started cleaning up the kitchen. Marcus frowned at Bruce. Bruce shook his head in hopes the other man wouldn't say anything.

He got up and carried his bowl and plate to the sink. When she took them to wash, he laid a hand on her shoulder and bent over to whisper in her ear.

"Thanks for moving our things for us." He hoped she would understand he meant thanks for not getting rid of Irene's things.

"Sure." She shrugged. "Everything's just like I found it."

She had understood. He felt like a heel now that he'd said something. Why hadn't he just left things like they were? He sighed and walked back to the table to join the discussion. When the conversation began to ebb, he stood up and stretched.

"Time for bed. I'll add more wood to the fire, Mike." Bruce walked into the living room and worked on the fire.

Mike eased back into the living room and on the couch. "I should be able to walk around more tomorrow. I'm feeling a lot better now that I've gotten up."

"Just don't go too fast and have a relapse." Bruce patted the man's good shoulder.

"I won't. I just think I need to leave as soon as I can and give you guys time to get to know my sister. She's not relaxing around you like she should. I think it's my fault."

"Don't you worry about her. We'll work it out between us soon enough. It just takes time to find yourself in a new place. She is having to do it for the second time in a year."

Mike just nodded and settled under the covers.

Kate walked into the room and hugged and kissed Mike good night. "If you need anything, just call up the stairs. We'll hear you."

"I'll be fine. I can get up and down by myself now if I need anything. Don't worry about me, Kate."

"Come on, baby." Marcus wrapped an arm around her shoulders and drew her toward the stairs.

Kate climbed them with Bruce bringing up the rear. Her twitching ass had his cock growing harder by the second. Fuck, he wanted that ass, but she wasn't anywhere near ready for that. Instead, he needed to be concentrating on making her feel good so she would relax around them.

As soon as they entered the bedroom, Bruce closed the door and began undressing. Marcus did the same. Only Kate stood still without pulling off her clothes. She seemed scared to move.

"What is it, baby?" Bruce asked.

"Um, I was going to take a shower. I'll be back in a few minutes." She headed for the bathroom.

"We're going to take one, too, baby. It's a big walk-in. We can all fit." Bruce watched her eyes grow wide.

"Oh, um, I can take a bath if you two want the shower." She was backpedaling, trying to get out of it.

"Naw, we'll all three bathe together."

He walked over and began undressing her. She took over unfastening her pants. Once Marcus had her shirt off, she bent over and pulled off her jeans. Then she stepped out of her underwear as he pulled off her bra. She stood there with her hands by her side, obviously trying not to cover herself.

Marcus urged her toward the bathroom. He turned on the shower, adjusting the water temperature before stepping inside.

"Come on, Kate. It's warm enough. You're going to catch a chill in the cool air."

Bruce sat out the towels and grabbed a couple of washcloths. He planned for them to bathe her. Marcus smiled, taking the hint, and rinsed out his cloth to start on her face.

"Hey, I can bathe myself, guys."

"But we want to bathe you, Kate. Just relax and let us take care of you." Marcus began soaping up the cloth and running it up and down her arm.

Bruce did the same thing and washed her other arm. They each took a side and bathed her from top to bottom. He liked that her face grew red when they each took a breast to clean. He rinsed her off and bent over her to suck on her nipple. Marcus followed his lead and they were both drawing tightly at her tits.

When she moaned, he reached between her legs to find her wet, and not from the shower. Her silken juices were coating his fingers as he played with her pussy. He could take her now, and she'd be ready for him. If he did, Marcus could take her later when they were in bed. He knew he was just making excuses for having sex with her, but he wanted her. He didn't want to wait.

He pulled her to him and kissed her. He licked along the seam of her mouth in an effort to gain entrance. She slowly opened her mouth to his and he attacked her with his lips, teeth, and tongue. He couldn't get enough of her. She tasted spicy like the chili. Marcus was nibbling at her neck from behind. No doubt his cock was poking at her ass like his was poking at her belly. Did it excite her or scare her? He pulled back to see her face.

Her eyes were shuttered in arousal. It was all he needed to see. He grasped her leg and held it while he fit his cock to her slit. Marcus held her steady with his hands on her breasts from behind her.

Bruce thrust into her as she let her head fall back against Marcus's chest. She moaned when he pulled out and thrust again. It took three tries before he had seated himself against her cervix. He held himself still for a few seconds as he regained control. Then slowly moved in and out of her until she was holding on to him in an effort to keep him seated inside of her.

Marcus continued his assault on her nipples as he kissed, licked, and sucked along her shoulder and neck.

Kate whimpered when he pulled out and pushed back in again. He slowly began to increase his pace and the strength of his thrusts until only Marcus holding her up kept her off the back of the shower wall. He could feel his balls draw up and cursed that he couldn't prolong his climax any longer. What was it about her that squeezed his dick dry every time he got inside of her?

He reached between them and fingered her clit as he tunneled in and out of her hot cunt. She started to scream, and Marcus took her mouth, smothering her screams even as she climaxed around Bruce's pulsing cock. He shot cum deep into her pussy. He held himself there inside her cunt while he emptied himself. He finally let her leg down and all but collapsed against the side wall while trying to catch his breath.

She leaned back into Marcus. He rubbed her belly in soft circles while whispering how good she was in her ear.

After a few seconds she seemed to have caught her breath. She surprised them both by going down on her knees and taking Marcus's cock in her hands. She squeezed him then licked around the slit in the top, making his brother come up on his toes.

"Fuck, baby. That feels good."

Bruce watched as she circled the mushroom head with her tongue before sucking in just the head. His cock began to grow again at the sight of her taking his brother's cock deep into her mouth. When she took him deep in her throat, he nearly groaned out loud like Marcus did.

Instead, he grasped his own cock and stroked it as she sucked on Marcus. The noises she was making around his cock drove Bruce wild with need. She alternated between deep-throating and shallow bobbing until Marcus was holding her head and face-fucking her. He held her hand at the base of him so he wouldn't choke her.

Bruce grinned when she reached between his brother's legs and grasped his balls. She gently rolled them in her hand, causing him to shout out and go up on his toes once again.

"Fuck, like that, baby. Just like that. God, I'm going to come, Kate. If you don't want it, you need to back off, baby."

She swallowed him down again, and Marcus exploded in her mouth. Her throat worked at swallowing his cum. Bruce watched until she pulled off of Marcus and licked the remaining cum from his cock.

He continued to stroke his cock in long pulls as she glanced in his direction. Her mouth formed a tiny *O*. She looked up at his face and bit her lower lip at whatever she saw in his eyes.

"Suck my cock, Kate. I want to feel that hot mouth around my dick."

She licked her lips with her tiny pink tongue and leaned in his direction. He met her halfway and groaned when she licked the drop of pre-cum from the slit in the top of his dick. She licked all around his hard cockhead. Then she sucked just below the head on the rim, driving him to his toes. She sucked hard on his cock until she sucked him down her throat. There she swallowed around him and hummed against his dick.

"Fuck, just like that, baby." He couldn't keep his hands off her.

Bruce wound his hands in her hair and thrust into her mouth. She groaned around him then swallowed again.

"Aw, baby. Yes, do it again." She swallowed around him and he knew he was a goner.

She squeezed his balls, and despite having just come only minutes earlier, he shot cum down her throat. Neither one of them were ready. She choked but swallowed then came up off him with her teeth barely grazing his cock when she did. It sent chills down his spine.

"Kate, that was un-fucking-believable." He pulled her to her feet and shoved her against the back of the shower where he could eat at her mouth and jaw.

He didn't give a fuck that his cum had just been there. Hell, it didn't even matter that his brother's had been there before his. He had to kiss her, had to taste her skin. She shivered as he held her head still for his assault.

"Bruce, man. I think she's getting cold. The water is cold now." Marcus stood at the opening holding a towel. He was wearing his thermal bottoms.

"Fuck, Kate. I'm sorry. Let's get you warm." He helped her out of the shower and grabbed another towel to dry off with while Marcus took care of her.

He couldn't stop watching her face as she struggled to regain control of her breathing. He wasn't in much better shape himself. He finally dragged his gaze from hers and located his thermals. He needed to get a grip. Let Marcus cuddle her and take care of her. He didn't need to get so attached to her. He would never be able to do what was right to keep her safe if he let his heart lead the way.

They all three climbed into bed and curled up together to keep warm under the blankets. He felt Kate's cold nose burrow into his chest. He growled at her, but she didn't move it. In truth, he didn't want her to.

Marcus looked over her shoulder at him with a questioning expression on his face. Bruce just shook his head. He would talk to him in the morning when they were away from Kate. He wanted to make sure that Marcus gave her whatever she needed emotionally, because he wasn't going to be able to.

Even if he wanted to let his heart get involved, he was afraid it was locked up with Irene deep in the ground. Yet lying there in bed, he wasn't able to bring up her face in his mind. It bothered him. He sighed and gave up after a few minutes.

"Bruce? Are you okay?"

"Yeah, I'm fine."

"Get some rest. We've got a long winter ahead of us," Marcus said.

"Right. Good night, Marcus."

Chapter Thirteen

Two weeks later, Mike was getting ready to head back to his place. Kate didn't want him to leave, but understood he was ready to go. She was sure being around the men who were having sex with his sister was beginning to take its toll on him. As much as she tried to be quiet, they drove her crazy with their hands and mouths.

"We're just a few miles away, Mike. You can come over anytime you want to." Kate didn't even check to be sure it was okay with the guys. It was fine with her. He was her brother.

"You can come see me anytime, too, Kate. Just remember not to come on your own. It's too dangerous even in a truck."

"I know, Mike. I'll bring one of the guys with me when I visit. You're sure you have plenty of food there?"

"Kate, stop worrying about me. Without you there, there's twice as much as I need. I'll be fine." He climbed up into the truck and started it up.

"Thanks for taking care of me, guys. I'll check in with you from time to time. If you need me for anything, you know where I am."

"Just remember what I said about the snow. It'll be deep this time, so keep it shoveled away from the door."

Mike nodded and backed out of their drive, turning around in the yard and heading off to his place, without her.

Kate couldn't stop the tears from falling as the truck disappeared around a curve. He was all she had left of her family, and now he was gone as well.

"Aw, Kate. Don't cry. He's just down the road a piece. We can go see him, and he can come see you." Marcus hugged her.

"Let her cry, Marcus. Things are changing and she knows it." Bruce brushed a kiss across her cheek and walked inside.

Marcus stayed outside with her while she struggled to regain her composure. He hugged and kissed her and rubbed his cheek against hers. Kate sniffed and stood up straight.

"I better get inside and start dinner. I thought I would make a meatloaf and mashed potatoes."

"Sounds good, baby." Marcus opened the door for her.

Kate had postponed Mike leaving until the night before it was supposed to start snowing. She had wanted as much time with him there as possible. Even though she was content with Bruce and Marcus, she would miss her brother. She knew that once he was gone, everything would be different. Deep down she knew they would never hurt her, but part of her was still uneasy around them. They were just so big.

Marcus left her in the kitchen and joined Bruce in the living room. No doubt they would discuss the cattle and the coming snow. They were serious that this snow would be deep. Bruce worried about the wind, saying it would build drifts over the windows if they let it.

"Kate!" Bruce called from the other room.

She walked into the living room, drying her hands as she did. "Yeah?"

"When you get the food in the oven, come sit with us for a while, baby."

"Um, okay. I'll be back in a few minutes." She gave them a shaky smile and retreated to the kitchen once again.

As soon as she had the potatoes boiled waiting for her to mash them and the meatloaf in the oven, she washed her hands and left her apron in the kitchen so that she could sit with her men. She expected them to sit on the couch in front of the fireplace, but Bruce called her over to his recliner.

She climbed up and he settled her on his lap. He was hard already. What did that mean? Did he want her to suck him off right there?

With Marcus, she always knew what he was thinking, but with Bruce, she was in the dark. He didn't show his emotions like his brother did.

"We wanted to talk to you, Kate," Marcus began.

"The wolves are dangerous. They nearly killed a couple of the women around here. Some of the men are getting together to hunt them down and thin them out. We're probably going to go in with them. We were waiting for Mike to get ready to go home. He's not able to join us, but he would have wanted to." Bruce ran a hand down her arm then back up again.

"Thanks for thinking about that. I would have worried myself sick with him out there and you, too." She swallowed and turned to look up at him. "When are you going to go?"

"Tomorrow, provided the snow hasn't gotten too deep to walk in. We're taking you with us to stay at one of the houses with the other women."

"Surely I could just stay here. I don't know these other women."

"Baby, you'll enjoy being around other women. Several of them are pregnant, and it will help them to feel less anxious." Marcus smiled at her.

"You'll go and stay with the other women, Kate. It's safest, and you'll do what's safe."

She drew in a deep breath and let it out slowly. Nodding her head, she waited for whatever was next.

"Remember that you are not to ever go outside without one of us with you. The house better be on fire if I ever catch you outside alone. It's for your safety, Kate." Bruce's voice was stern.

Kate had no intentions of going outside alone. Just the knowledge that their first wife had been attacked and killed by wolves was enough reason for her.

"I won't go outside for any reason, Bruce."

"Good girl." He squeezed her against him.

"As soon as the snows clear, we'll go to one of the cities and see about getting you some pretty clothes to wear."

"What's wrong with what I've got?" She knew they were mostly work clothes, but why dress up out in the middle of nowhere?

"Nothing, baby," Marcus assured her. "We just want to see you in something frilly sometimes."

"Nothing wrong with wearing a dress now and then," Bruce said.

"Okay." She knew she wasn't small like their Irene had been, but dressing her up wasn't going to change anything. She just wasn't Irene. "I better go check dinner."

Bruce nodded and helped her down. She hurried to the kitchen before her tears would be seen by Marcus. She didn't want them to know that they had hurt her feelings. She was sure they hadn't meant to. She didn't need to let anything they said upset her. It wasn't like she loved them or anything, right?

Kate checked the meatloaf then drained the potatoes so she could mash them. She poured some of the milk from the cow into the boiler and began to mash them with the potato masher. By the time she had her feelings under control again, the potatoes were free of lumps and ready to eat.

She pulled the meatloaf from the oven and called the men into eat. They consumed their meal with as much relish as they always did, but Marcus kept looking at her funny. She smiled at him and continued to pick at her food. She ate a good bit, she thought, but when she stood up to clear her plate, Bruce stopped her.

"Eat some more, Kate. All you did was pick at your food."

"I'm not hungry, Bruce."

"Kate, eat. You have to keep up your strength. It's cold now, but it's going to get colder in the next few days. Eat."

She sat back down and forced more of the meatloaf and potatoes down. Marcus smiled at her in encouragement.

When she got up the second time, Bruce didn't say anything. He got up as well and raked his plate out along with hers. He and Marcus disappeared into the living room once again, and she cleaned up the kitchen. She was exhausted with everything that had gone on that day.

If she was going to meet some other women, she needed to be at her best tomorrow.

Kate walked into the living room where the conversation between the two men stopped at her entrance.

"I'm going to go on to bed. I'm tired."

"Do you need help in the bathroom, Kate?" Marcus asked.

"No, thanks. I'm just going to take a quick shower and climb into bed."

"We'll be up in a few minutes, Kate," Bruce told her.

"'Night." She climbed the stairs and hurried into the bathroom to finish her shower before they arrived.

She really didn't feel like sex tonight. They would want it, though. Well, if she didn't feel like it, they would have to do without.

Thirty minutes later, she had just climbed into bed when they walked in the door. They quickly removed their clothes and disappeared in the bathroom for twenty minutes. Then they returned, drying off as they slipped into bed without their thermals.

"Um, Marcus?"

"Yeah, baby." He nuzzled her neck while his hard cock pressed against her side.

"I don't feel real well tonight."

"Do you feel sick?" Bruce asked next to her ear.

"Not sick really, just not well."

"Kate. If you don't want to have sex, you can just tell us," Bruce said. "We're grown men."

"I really don't feel well. I think it's just all the buildup of Mike leaving."

"You felt safe with Mike here, and now with him gone, you don't anymore. Is that it?" Bruce sat up on one elbow and looked down at her.

She turned her eyes to Marcus then back to Bruce. How had he known? Was she that obvious?

"I know you won't hurt me. I'm just not real comfortable around you yet, I guess. Please don't be mad."

"We're not mad, baby. Always be honest with us about how you feel." Marcus kissed her softly on the lips.

"Bruce?" She was scared about how he felt. He was the one who she was the most uncomfortable around.

"Marcus is right. Always be honest about your feelings with us. If we aren't honest with each other, we'll grow to resent one another."

It was on the tip of her tongue to ask him about Irene then, but she realized he hadn't been dishonest with her. He hadn't told her he loved her, or even that he cared about her, as Marcus had done. It hurt, but she understood.

"What's the sad face for, baby?" Marcus squeezed her thigh.

"Nothing. I guess I'm thinking about Mike being all alone tonight."

"He'll be fine," Marcus assured her.

"Get some sleep, Kate. Tomorrow will be a long day for you." Bruce patted her arm and turned over to go to sleep.

* * * *

When Kate got out of bed the next morning it was to the knowledge that the men had left her to sleep in. She looked out the window and found a white blanket of snow on the ground below her. She hurried into her clothes and ran down the stairs. She knew the men were already gone by the missing coats and boots at the back door. She warmed up coffee and fixed some eggs to eat. She wanted to go outside, but knew she couldn't Instead, she watched out the window for the men to return. They said they were going over to the other men's house around two so they would need to come back soon to get ready. She warmed up some chili and let it simmer while she waited.

Around noon, they crunched through the snow onto the back porch. She waited until they had stomped off the snow then removed their coats before asking about how it was out there.

"Snow's deep, but not too bad. We can walk around in it fairly well. It will be hard enough to give the wolves some trouble, though." Bruce quickly crossed to the washroom to clean up.

Marcus was close behind him. "Probably going to get more snow tonight, though, so today will be the best time to go after them."

"How many are going hunting?" she asked.

"I think there will be ten of us. Two of the men will stay behind with the women. You'll be staying in their cellar for safety."

"The cellar? Why would we need to stay in the cellar?" Surely they were going overboard.

"Last time the wolves attacked one of the houses and got in by jumping through one of the windows. We're not taking any more chances," he said.

Kate shivered. "They actually attacked a house? What is going on with them? They're supposed to be afraid of men."

"They've had this area of the nation to themselves for nearly six years, and now we're taking it back one little piece at a time. They're getting smart and banding together to hunt us even as we hunt them." Bruce pulled her into his arms and hugged her tightly. "Just promise me you'll mind whoever they leave behind and stay in the cellar with the other women."

"Okay, I promise." She didn't want to be around wolves that were that smart anyway.

"Let's eat. I'm starved," Marcus said.

Once they were finished eating and the dishes had been washed, dried, and put away, Kate dressed in her warmest clothes and bundled up to ride to someone's house she didn't know.

"We're going to Garrett, Brice, and Ronnie's house. It's about thirty minutes from here. Ronnie is pregnant, as is another woman,

Heather. Her men are Brandon and Bolton. I don't know the other men and women who will be there," Marcus told her.

As soon as they pulled into the drive, the door opened to the house and a giant of a man walked out. He waited until they had gotten out of the truck before he stepped off the porch into the snow.

"I'm Garrett. You must be Marcus and Bruce." He smiled down at Kate. She hid behind the men. "You have to be Kate. It's great to meet you all. Come on in and meet the rest of the group."

They followed the big man inside the house. Instantly she felt a kinship with the women. They were all with two men. Maybe Mike had been right. Maybe the only way to keep a woman safe in this new world they were in was to share her between more than one man. Though the living area was huge, the room was crammed full of people. She wrapped her arms around Marcus's waist and buried her face in his back.

"Come on, Kate. Let's settle you into the kitchen with the rest of the women." Bruce followed the women as they filed into the kitchen. He gently pushed Kate along behind them. "We'll just be in the other room, baby. Don't worry. I won't leave without saying good-bye and seeing you into the cellar."

Kate nodded and spared a quick glance at where Marcus was talking to one of the other men. He smiled in her direction when his eyes met hers. Then the other women were drawing her into their conversation.

"I'm Heather, and this is Jessie," one of the women said. She was quite pregnant with a rounded belly that stuck out. Jessie smiled at her.

"I'm Ronnie. It's great to meet you. The more of us women the better. All that testosterone is overwhelming at times," she said.

"I'm Leigh." Another woman held out her hand, and Kate shook it.

Kate noticed she, Heather, and Ronnie all had scars or fresh wounds on their hands. She figured they went further up their arms as well.

Ronnie noticed she was staring at their arms. "We were attacked a few weeks back, and they got to us."

"Bruce was telling me about it. I'm sorry. Everyone's okay, right?"

"Yes, we're all okay." She pointed out Heather. "Heather was attacked in their backyard last year when she went to tend to the chickens. She was nearly killed."

"I'm glad you're okay. That had to have been horrible."

"I'm lucky that I don't remember much of it," the other woman said.

"Okay, ladies. Let's get you in the cellar." Jonathan, one of Leigh's husbands, herded them toward the open pantry door and down into the cellar.

"I'm Jonathan, and this is Wyatt. We'll be down here with you until the others get back."

"Wyatt's mine," Jessie said with a smile.

They all gathered on blankets in a circle. The men covered them with more blankets. Kate looked toward the door. Bruce and Marcus had promised to say good-bye before they left. She waited, and sure enough, all the men piled down the stairs to tell their women good-bye. Bruce and Marcus walked over and knelt beside her.

"We'll be back in a few hours, baby. Stay warm and safe for us," Marcus told her. He kissed her. Then Bruce squeezed her shoulder and they filed back up the stairs.

Jonathan locked the door and placed a brace across it. She shuddered at the thought that they needed so much security. It didn't seem real that a bunch of wolves could attack a house and get inside. But she was sitting among a group of woman where over half of them had been harmed by wolves.

The woman talked among themselves about cooking and their gardens. Kate listened mostly. She was new to all of this and had not even been out there a full year. When Ronnie realized she was a newlywed, as they all called it, she began to tell her all the things she needed to be prepared for. The list was daunting.

Then they heard the howls.

Chapter Fourteen

As soon as the men were all back in the house, they knocked on the cellar door to let the others know they could come out. Bruce and Marcus waited impatiently to see Kate emerge from the depths of the cellar unharmed.

Bruce and Marcus knew none of the wolves had gotten in the house, but a sense of urgency had them grabbing Kate and pulling her back into their arms just the same.

"Did you get any of them?" Ronnie asked Brice.

"We managed to kill about seven of them, but there are plenty more. It's almost as if all the wolves from the area are converging. Damndest thing I've ever seen."

"No one was hurt?" Jonathan asked.

"No, there were a couple of close calls, but with this many men, it was hard for them to try and cut any of us out to attack," Kent explained.

"Bruce, Marcus, we really appreciate your joining up with us. You're both damn good shots." Bolton shook their hands around Kate. She seemed to have been fine with the women downstairs, but now she acted as if she wanted to go home.

"Just let us know when you want to hunt again. We're headed home. I want to get Kate out of the cold as soon as I can." Bruce shook the other men's hands as they headed for the door.

Marcus kept his arm around Kate's shoulders as they walked outside and headed for the truck. All the way down the drive to where Bruce had parked, Kate kept turning her head this way and that trying to see around them.

"What is it, Kate?" Bruce finally asked.

"I just feel like someone is watching us."

"I'm sure the guys from the house are making sure we get to the truck safely."

She sighed. Bruce was sure she felt like they were ignoring her. Then as they opened the truck doors, a twig snapped.

"Fuck, get her in the truck, Marcus." Bruce climbed in and slammed his door.

Marcus shoved her inside and climbed in behind her. When he closed his door, it was just in time to keep a wolf from snatching at his leg. The dark brown animal growled at them before backing into the woods once again.

"Damn, that was close." Bruce looked at Kate. "Next time you think someone is watching, tell us to remember this."

"Don't worry. I will." She hugged herself.

Marcus kissed her cheek then fastened her safety belt and hugged her to him as Bruce backed them out of the drive. The thirty plus minutes it took them to get back to the house was made in silence. Bruce was still shaking on the inside from the near miss earlier. If the wolf had gotten Marcus out of the truck, another one would have gotten to Kate. He had misjudged their intelligence—again.

As soon as they pulled into the drive, Bruce was issuing orders.

"I'm going to go unlock the door. Don't get out of the truck until I can cover you with the gun, Marcus. Keep Kate close to you."

"Got it. I'll take care of her." Marcus was unbuckling her seat belt.

Bruce climbed out of the driver's side of the truck with his rifle in his hand. He hurried to the front door and unlocked it, checking the house to make sure all the doors and windows were intact. When he didn't find anything to worry about, he walked back to the front door and nodded at Marcus.

While Marcus quickly walked Kate to the door, Bruce scanned the tree line on both sides of the house for any sign of a wolf. As soon as his brother and their wife were inside, he stepped back inside and closed the door, locking it in the process.

He pulled Kate from Marcus's arms and squeezed her into his. He didn't want to bury another wife. The intelligence of the animals was uncanny.

"Bruce, you're hurting me." Kate's strained voice cut into his thoughts.

He let her go after kissing the top of her head. "Sorry. I wasn't thinking."

"I'm fine, Bruce. Nothing happened." She smiled up at him.

He tried to temper his thoughts and smile back at her, but it must have been a sad smile, because she pursed her lips and nodded before backing away.

"I'm going to go fix us something to eat. I'm sure you're starved." Kate disappeared into the kitchen, leaving him and Marcus to discuss the hunt.

"Keeping her safe is the most important thing we have to do, Marcus. One of us is to stay with her at all times once spring gets here. She'll be safe enough in the house, I think. I don't think the wolves will attack the house when we aren't actively hunting them. I can't believe they have that much intelligence." Bruce looked out at the front yard and the fast approaching night.

"I agree. I'm going to check the animals real quick before she gets dinner ready." Marcus stood up and grabbed his rifle.

"Be careful. Don't take any chances." Bruce clapped his brother on the shoulder.

"I don't plan to."

Bruce followed Marcus through to the kitchen and watched as he shoved his hands into his coat and his feet into his other boots. Then he closed the door behind him.

"Where is Marcus going?" Kate asked as she stirred something in a bowl.

"To check on the animals before we eat." He walked over to peer over her shoulder.

"What are we eating tonight?"

"Potato patties, fried deer steak, and green beans."

"Sounds good. I'm going to go ahead and take a shower. If you hear anything outside, come get me immediately. Don't open the door."

"Okay." She nodded and continued stirring.

Bruce sighed and walked out of the kitchen. He knew he was losing Kate over to Marcus, but that was how it needed to be. He climbed the stairs and walked into the bedroom. He pulled out clean clothes then turned on the shower and adjusted the water. Tonight they would take her together. They had been preparing her for the last two weeks. It was time. It would be one of the few ways he could connect to her and keep his heart intact. Sex with Kate was an amazing thing.

He quickly bathed and dried off. Once he had his clothes on, he hurried downstairs to see if Marcus was back yet. He found them together in the kitchen. Marcus had her in his arms, kissing her as if nothing else mattered in the world. Right then, it probably didn't. Bruce backed out of the room and settled in his recliner. They would call when the food was on the table. Until then, he'd take a short nap.

Only all he could think about was seeing his brother's arms around Kate and wanting to be with them. No, he wouldn't risk something happening to Kate like it had Irene because he'd been too wrapped up in her. If he hadn't loved Irene so much, he would have been aware of the dangers around them and she never would have been left alone that day.

* * * *

As soon as the dishes were washed and put away, Bruce herded her upstairs with him and Marcus. He was especially on edge tonight, and she was sure hunting the wolves had upset him. He kept a hand on her ass the entire trip up the stairs.

"Marcus, bathe her while I get ready and pull back the covers." Marcus smiled a long, slow smile at that.

Kate wasn't sure what was going on, but pulling back the covers meant sex and a cold bed. Anticipation began to gather in her womb. Her nipples peaked at the thought of what they would do to her tonight. She never knew what to expect. But she was always well satisfied.

"Come on, Kate. I'll scrub your back for you." Marcus pulled her into the bathroom and shut the door to keep the warm air from the shower circulating inside the room.

He quickly stripped them both and, after adjusting the water temperature, pulled her into the shower. She laughed when he got a face full of water for his efforts.

"Serves you right. Don't pull me around like a rag doll." She washed her face then soaped up the cloth and began to bathe Marcus.

"Turn around, Kate, and let me scrub your back and shoulders." He soaped her up with the cloth and then massaged her into a wet noodle with his bare hands. When he let go of her, she nearly collapsed. He chuckled and turned her around to rinse off.

They quickly finished showering then stepped out and dried off. Marcus wrapped his arms around her and kissed her forehead.

"Baby, we're going to love you together tonight. Are you ready?"

"Together? What do you mean?" She was sure she knew, but wanted Marcus to explain it to her.

"I'm going to fuck that sweet pussy of yours while Bruce takes your ass. It will be the best thing you've ever felt before, baby. I promise."

"It will hurt, Marcus." She was scared, but curious at the same time.

Almost every time that Bruce had played with her back hole he'd made her feel good while he did it, but there was always the pinch and burn at first. Taking a cock in her ass would mean a lot of pinch and burn. She shivered.

"It only burns for a few seconds, baby. You remember how good it felt for him to fuck you there with his fingers. You climax hard when he does that with me inside you. Just relax and push back for him, baby. We wouldn't hurt you for the world, Kate."

"I know. I'm just nervous."

Marcus pulled her tighter in his arms and kissed her gently on the lips. His tongue licked around her lips then, when she opened them, licked inside her mouth. Their tongues moved against each other and tangled together until a knock at the door pulled them apart.

"Coming, Bruce." Marcus winked at her. "He's anxious. He can't wait to get inside that tight ass of yours."

They walked out into the chilly bedroom. Marcus hurried her over to the bed. Bruce climbed on top of her back and began rubbing her skin with something that felt warm and tingly all at the same time.

"What is that?" she asked.

"A menthol lotion. It will help keep you warm all over." He finished rubbing it into her back, arms, and ass cheeks then moved down her legs. "Roll over for me, baby."

Bruce skipped her breasts, but rubbed it into her belly and down the front of her legs as well. Then he put the lotion up and leaned over to lick and nip at her nipples. Marcus took one into his mouth and began sucking on it while Bruce slipped a finger between her pussy lips into her slit. He delved inside with one finger then added a second one. When he pulled out, she whimpered.

"Easy, baby. I'm going to have some of your sweet cream for dessert."

While Marcus continued manipulating and licking her breasts, Bruce moved down her body until he could shoulder her legs wide apart. Then he spread her pussy lips and stabbed her with his stiffened tongue. She shuddered all over as he fucked her with it over and over.

His thumbs circled her back hole until she wanted to scream for him to fuck her there. The anticipation was driving her crazy.

He stopped fucking her with his tongue and licked instead. He dragged his tongue from the bottom of her slit to the top right over her clit. She shuddered and lifted her hips in an effort to keep his rasping tongue on her little button. Instead, he pulled back and began pumping two fingers in and out of her cunt. He curved them and found that little spot deep inside of her that sent her flying with each stroke.

"God, you're tight, baby." Bruce grinned up at Marcus. "Wait until you get inside of her, Marcus. She's squeezing my fingers like Vise-Grip pliers."

Marcus hummed around a nipple, sending shivers down her spine. He nipped at one and twisted the other as she cried out at the amazing sensation. Her nipples were supersensitive, and Marcus knew just what to do to get her to come.

Bruce began to lap at her pussy like a cat licking milk. She thrashed her head from side to side, needing more from them. She needed that little bite of pain that she got when Marcus twisted or pinched her nipples or Bruce fingered her ass. She tried lifting her pelvis to give him more room to get to her, but he put a hand on her belly and kept her flat on the bed.

"Easy, Kate. I'll take care of you. Let me have my fun first." Bruce's voice sounded strained for a change.

"Please, Bruce. I need to come. I can't stand it." She hated to beg.

"In a bit, baby. Just relax and let it find you." He continued licking and stroking her pussy until she was crying with need.

Finally, he pressed on her hot spot and sucked in her clit all at the same time. Marcus pinched and twisted her nipples. They sent her screaming over the edge. Even before she was fully recovered, Marcus had her climbing on top of him. He steadied her with one hand and held his cock still for her to sit on with the other.

As she drew him into her body, she couldn't help but moan at the fullness. Her cunt was still swollen from coming, and his thick dick had to work its way inside of her. She panted then sighed when he finally reached the end of her. She leaned over him and took his mouth in a kiss. It left her ass free for Bruce to play with.

She felt him rub lube around her back hole and begin to prepare her for his fingers. First he entered her with one finger and fucked her with it. Then he added the second finger. This one pinched a little, but nothing major. She fucked herself up and down on Marcus's cock, stabbing herself with Bruce's fingers on each downward stroke.

When he pulled out, she expected three fingers, but instead, he added more lube, and his massive cock pushed against her back hole. She gasped in surprise and clamped down on Marcus's dick.

"Easy, baby. Relax and push out, remember?" he asked.

Kate nodded and concentrated on relaxing her body. Then she pushed out until the burning began, and a tight pinch signaled he'd pushed through the resistant ring. He drove deep inside her ass then stilled for her to get used to him being there.

She panted around the pain then squirmed as she began to want to move—needed to move. The pressure was almost too much as Bruce's sweaty forehead rubbed against her back. He was trying to give her time, but it was hard on him. She knew this, knew that he was anxious to move as much as she was.

Kate tried to pull back from Marcus and bury Bruce deeper in her ass, but she didn't have the strength to do it.

"Please, Bruce, move. I can't stand it. Someone move!" She pressed her forehead into Marcus's chest.

Bruce pulled out, and Marcus lifted her with the force of his push inside of her. He bumped her cervix, adding to the mix of pleasure and pain that was swirling inside of her. Then he pulled out, and Bruce thrust in. They slowly fucked her, alternating in and out until she was wild with need. She needed them to go faster, deeper. She whimpered as nerve endings came alive and stoked her climax higher and higher as they shifted in and out of her body.

Kate's body wasn't her own anymore. They controlled it as they burrowed in and out of her over and over again. Fire burned inside her cunt as her climax began to grow closer to the surface. Marcus's dick scraped over her G-spot with nearly every thrust. It tightened muscles all along her thighs, ass, and pelvis. The rasp of Marcus's chest hair against her highly sensitized nipples was just one more sensation that soon had her screaming as the men pummeled her with their cocks. Her pussy and ass tightened around them until they were cursing their climaxes along with hers.

She screamed as she came. Her heart beat as fast as a machine gun's fire, and her breathing became so labored she thought she would suffocate. Her ears began to ring, and she felt the hot fire of their cum coating her ass and her cunt as they came. Then she felt and knew nothing.

Chapter Fifteen

Kate woke to find herself being submerged in a hot tub of water. Marcus held her in his arms as Bruce sat her in it. She moaned at the wonderful feel of it on her body. She thought every muscle in her body was probably sore from her climax. It had taken her over when she came.

"Hey there, sleepyhead. How do you feel?"

"Tired." She closed her eyes again.

"No you don't," Bruce said. "Stay awake long enough for us to bathe you."

She opened her eyes and glared at him. He just chuckled and began to wash her body with the soft, soapy cloth. She was slick with sweat and other body fluids. The bath actually felt great. She struggled to sit up on Marcus's lap. He grunted when her hip made contact with his already stiffened cock.

She frowned. "Don't you ever go down?" she asked the men as she noticed that Bruce was in the same condition.

Bruce chuckled. "Not around you, we don't."

"Hell, I don't even go down when I'm out working the cattle if I'm thinking about you," Marcus said.

"God, that has to be, um, hard to deal with." She smiled at her own pun.

"Smart-ass. I'll take care of that smart mouth of yours if you're not careful. I'll fill it with my dick." Bruce stood up and the cock in question bobbed up and down with the movement.

"Now that will really punish me." She licked her lips and smiled up at him.

Something passed over his face that worried her. He seemed to be struggling with something. What was it? Before she could ask him, Marcus pronounced her clean and shoved her to a standing position. Bruce grabbed her by the shoulders to keep her on her feet.

"Easy, Marcus. We don't want her to fall," Bruce chided his brother.

"Sorry." He just grinned up at Kate before he stood up as well.

Water poured from his body as he helped her out of the tub. Bruce dried her off while Marcus took care of himself. As soon as she was dry, he picked her up and carried her to the bed once again. The covers had been pulled back up to keep as much warmth as possible in the bed.

"Climb under the covers, baby. I'm right behind you." He slapped her ass once as she crawled under.

"Hey! What was that for?" She stuck her head back out, grinning at him.

"For being too slow."

"Asshole." She stuck her cold feet against his ass when he backed up to her.

"Kate, I'm going to spank that ass if you do that again."

Kate laughed and hugged up against his warm back. He seemed to radiate heat even in the winter. She buried her cold nose in his neck and heard him curse under his breath. She bit back another laugh in case it earned her the aforementioned spanking.

Marcus hurried across the cold floor and climbed into the bed on the other side of her. He snuggled up close to her back with his cold body. She shivered. Now she knew how poor Bruce felt. Marcus's hands were like ice cubes.

"Warm your hands up between your legs before you put them on me again," she fussed good-naturedly.

"I'm not putting my hands anywhere near my balls like this. I'll put them between your legs, though." He shoved them there, and she nearly came out of the bed in shock.

"Marcus, settle down and let's get some sleep. We have a lot to do tomorrow." Bruce sounded distracted.

"Is it supposed to snow more tomorrow?" she asked.

"Yeah, I bet we have another foot on the ground in the morning. It was starting to snow when we came up to bed."

Kate sighed. More snow meant more work on the men. They wouldn't let her help outside because of the wolves. Well, she would keep the fire going in the fireplace and food on the table. She could do that.

In that instant, she realized how much she had come to love being their wife even if Bruce didn't love her. She was almost sure Marcus did. She knew she loved him. She sighed. She even loved Bruce, but was sure he would never return the feeling. Still, in those few seconds when they were all three joined earlier, she had thought she heard him say the words in her ear. Now, though, she knew she had to have been mistaken.

* * * *

Over the next several weeks, they spent a lot of time in bed. When the men weren't out seeing to the animals, they were seeing to her in bed. Kate couldn't complain because she loved every minute of their attention. They loved her into blissful states where she dozed until they woke her again for more.

When she wasn't in bed with them, she cooked and cleaned. On several occasions during that time, one of the men from one of the other families stopped by to let them know what was going on. It seemed that the wolves had backed off somewhere. No one had seen a wolf since that last day of hunting. Everyone seemed to think that maybe they were retreating for good. Kate could tell that Bruce didn't believe it.

One day, Joel and Jonathan stopped by with Leigh to visit. She had only been out of bed for an hour and was still cleaning up after the men had eaten. They were outside with the cattle. She was afraid they would be mad if she let the other men inside. They seemed to understand, because they ushered Leigh in and walked around the house to find Bruce and Marcus.

"I'm sorry, Leigh. It's just that I don't know them and..."

"Don't worry about it. Joel would throw a fit if I let in a strange man even if there was a woman with them." She smiled and sat down at the kitchen table. "How are you doing?"

"I'm fine. I guess the snow has cleared up some if you are out in it."

"Yes, but then the guys have that big four-wheel drive with snow chains on the tires. I think they can go anywhere."

"How are the other women?" Kate asked.

"Everyone is fine. I think Heather is getting close to time to deliver. She's miserable, because she can't get comfortable."

"I can't even imagine being pregnant. That scares me to think about."

"Well, it's going to happen eventually. You've got two good men to help you, so you'll be fine."

A few minutes later, the men came stomping in the back door, pulling off boots and coats as they did. She and Leigh hurried to fix coffee for everyone. The men gathered in the living room. Marcus threw another log on the fire, and they continued their conversation as the women handed out the mugs of the steaming liquid.

"So you don't think the wolves are gone for good," Joel said.

"No, they're regrouping. I can't see them giving up as serious as they fought everyone these last two years. They're too smart. As long as man had the upper hand, they just used their intelligence to stay alive and hidden. Now that we're in the minority, they are pushing to take over the land."

"If I hadn't seen them in action I would think you were a nutcase, Bruce, but you're right. I don't see them giving up, either," Jonathan said as he sipped his coffee.

"I worry about the women," Joel said. "We have to work to put food on the table, and they have to work in the garden. Leigh can shoot a gun, but if she's busy in the yard, she might not see one in time."

"We've decided that one of us will always be with her outside. It means putting more on the other one, but I'm not leaving Kate alone." Bruce reached out and snagged her hand as she passed by to return to the kitchen.

Kate smiled down at him. He so rarely sought out her touch when sex wasn't involved. She squeezed his hand back. When he looked away and dropped her hand, she tried not to let it bother her. She continued into the kitchen where Leigh was back sitting at the table, stirring milk into her mug of caffeine.

"I think Joel wants to look at having a communal garden where we could all work with several of the men taking turns guarding us while we do. What do you think about that?"

"It sounds like a good idea. I don't know. It would need to be a big garden, and there would have to be set days we work in it so that everyone is there at the same time."

"I think it would work. That way only a couple of men a day would need to miss working in the fields or with the cattle." Leigh sipped her coffee.

"I wonder what Bruce and Marcus will think about it. I like the idea. Not only would it solve the problem of keeping us safe from the wolves, but it would mean we got to visit some every few days." Kate really liked the idea.

She hoped Bruce would go along with it. She knew Marcus would do whatever Bruce decided. Bruce made most of the decisions around the house, and they followed his directives.

A few minutes later, the men walked back into the kitchen. Jonathan and Joel pulled Leigh to her feet and the three of them put their boots, coats, and hats back on to leave.

Marcus walked them outside to their truck and then returned as Kate washed up the cups. He looked excited. For that matter, Bruce looked happy about something as well.

"What is it?" she finally asked when she couldn't stand it any longer.

"Don't act like you don't know, Kate. I'm sure Leigh said something to you. What do you think?" Bruce asked her.

Surprised, she opened then closed her mouth again. What should she say?

"I think it's a great idea. It would free you up to work without worrying about me, and I would get to visit with the other women some." She shrugged and grinned.

"I figured you would like the idea."

"You have to admit, it has merit," Marcus said.

"It will take at least one more family for it to be efficient."

"Do you think they will get the others to do it?" she asked.

"I don't know. Some of them are sure the wolves have moved on." Bruce shook his head.

"Even if they have, I think it's a good idea." Marcus wrapped his arms around Kate and pulled her back against him.

"Hey, let me finish drying the dishes." She reached for the last cup and after wiping it off, pulled Marcus behind her to the cabinet to put it up.

"There, you're finished. Let's go to bed."

"We haven't finished with the cattle, yet, Marcus," Bruce reminded him.

Kate leaned her head back and stuck out her tongue. He quickly sucked it into his mouth and teased her with his.

"Fuck you two. Go to bed. I'll tend to the last of the chores." Bruce shook his head and laughed as he pulled on his coat and boots. "I'll be back in another hour."

Marcus walked Kate toward the living room and the stairs. He pushed her up them as she laughed and tried to pull away from him.

Once they reached the top, he picked her up and carried her into the bedroom. They fell together on the bed and began pulling off each other's clothes.

Sex with Marcus was always fun and light or serious and sensual. With Bruce it was intense. He was always in control. Kate loved both of them and enjoyed their differences, but she especially liked it when they took her together. For a few minutes in time, they were joined, and no one was in control.

"I love you, Kate," Marcus said as he slowly entered her.

"I love you, Marcus." She drew in a deep breath as he filled her tight pussy with his hard cock.

He took her slow and deep with each rasp of his dick touching every part of her before it bumped against her cervix and shot pleasure down her spine. Slowly and methodically he pumped his cock in and out of her pussy.

"I can't get enough of you, Kate. God, you're so addicting."

Her juices coated his balls as he tunneled in and out of her, over and over in slow, measured thrusts designed to drive her higher and higher into ecstasy. With every thrust, she was sure it would be the one to send her screaming into orgasm, but still he pushed on.

"Fuck, you're so tight, baby." He licked a long line from her neck to her shoulder and bit her as he slowly picked up his speed.

Sweat dotted his forehead as he thrust his cock deeper and harder into her wet cunt. She held on to him, desperate to come now. She felt as if it would forever be out of her grasp now that he'd drawn it out for so long. Then he reached between them and tapped her clit as he bit her shoulder. She screamed as her orgasm exploded over her.

Nothing prepared her for the intense feeling of love she had for Marcus right then. He'd made love to her, showered her with attention and praise. Still, she wanted more. She wanted Bruce's love. She wanted to feel him deep within her when he said he loved her.

"I'm wasted," Marcus complained good-naturedly.

"So am I." She giggled then turned over in the bed and snuggled up to his back.

They lay like that for a long time, just dozing, until the opening of the door downstairs reminded them that Bruce would be wondering where they were. It had to have been over an hour now.

"Are you two still in bed?" he called up the stairs.

"I'm sorry, Bruce. I'll fix something to eat now." She grinned at Marcus and rolled out of bed to get dressed.

"You're both in hot water for wasting the day away in bed." Bruce was climbing the stairs.

"Hurry, up, Marcus!" Kate pulled on her T-shirt without bothering with a bra. She had all her clothes on when Bruce walked into the bedroom.

He shook his head and began pulling his off. "I'm going to take a shower. There better be something to eat on the table when I get downstairs, you two."

He slapped at her ass as she sprinted past him.

"Don't run down the stairs, Kate," he called after her.

Kate giggled and quickly walked down the stairs. She was bound and determined to get something for him to eat on the table before he made it downstairs. Marcus followed close behind her.

"What can I do to help?" he asked.

"Get out of my way." She slapped at his hands when they reached out to pluck at her nipples. The cool air in the house had them standing at attention. "Go on. Get out of my way."

He snuck in a kiss before hurrying into the living room. She heard the front door open and close. *He must have gone out to put a log on the fire.* She waited for him to return. When he didn't, she worried and walked to the front door. When she looked out, he was nowhere to be seen. She opened the door and called out to him, but he didn't answer. She stepped out onto the porch and listened. Still she could hear nothing. Then a twig snapped. Her mouth went dry, and her throat clogged with fear. She jumped back into the house and closed the door.

She ran around to the back to see if Marcus was out there, and there he was with the ax in his hand, walking toward the front door. He saw her looking out at him and waved. She waved back and worked at calming her racing heart. He would have known if there were wolves around. She was imagining things.

She swallowed around the slowly dissipating lump in her throat and started a boiler of soup. It was already made. She just had to warm it back up. She made crackling bread and sighed in relief when Marcus finally walked back in the house.

"Everything all right out there?" she asked.

"Everything's fine. Why?" He hung up his hat and coat.

"Just wondering. I have soup and crackling bread to eat. Do you think that will be okay with Bruce?"

"Bruce will let you know after he eats it." He stepped into the kitchen with still damp hair, wearing clean clothes.

After dinner, they gathered in the living room to talk and enjoy the fireplace. When Marcus went to get another log to put on the fire, Kate stopped him.

"Be careful. I think the wolves are still out there."

Bruce sat up and looked at her. "Why do you say that, Kate?"

"I just get this feeling that they are out there watching and waiting for us to make a wrong move."

"I'll watch for you, Marcus. We need to be especially careful at night." Bruce stood up and followed his brother to the door. After picking up the rifle, he opened the door and stood just outside waiting on Marcus to get the wood and bring it inside.

"Go ahead and get several logs, Marcus, so we will have them in the morning." Kate figured she could start the fire that way when she got up to start breakfast.

Once he had stacked three additional logs near the fireplace, they closed the door and Bruce put the rifle back where it belonged.

"I think it's time for us to go to bed. Kate, do you need to do anything in the kitchen first, baby?"

"No. I'm finished in there."

"Come on, then. I'm thinking of a word. Can you guess what it is?"

"Does it start with an *S*?" she asked, playing along.

"You got it, baby."

Chapter Sixteen

"What makes you think this is going to be the last snow of the season?" Kate asked Bruce.

"Just know. It probably won't last more than a couple of days, either. Just enough to be a nuisance, but not enough to do any real damage." Bruce grinned at her.

"Well, if it's the last one, I've got to make a snowman." She hadn't played out in the snow much at all over the winter because of the threat of the wolves and the fact that the men needed to work when they were out in the cold.

"We'll see, Kate. Depends on the weather. I'm not having you out in zero degree weather with the wind blowing. You'll catch your death like that." Bruce kissed the side of her face and continued to look out at the slowly falling snow while he drank his coffee.

Marcus walked down the stairs still tucking his shirttail into his jeans. He zipped and buttoned them when he reached the living room. Kate walked over and wrapped her arms around his waist.

"If Bruce says it's okay, I get to make a snowman later. You want to be my model?"

"Sure, baby. I'll be your model. If it doesn't snow any more than he thinks it is you won't be making a tall, dark, handsome one like me, though. You'll be making a short, squat one like Bruce."

"I heard that, brother."

Kate giggled and let go of Marcus to get him a mug of coffee, too. She returned from the kitchen with it a few seconds later to find them deep in conversation. She frowned but left Marcus's cup on the coffee table and returned to the kitchen. She looked out the window and watched as the snowflakes grew bigger and fell faster. Maybe there would be enough snow after all. She clapped her hands together and rummaged around in the pantry for an old carrot and some ruined potatoes for eyes. She cut the last one up to make his mouth.

"Kate, baby?" Bruce called her from the other room.

She hurried into the living room to find them waiting on her.

"If there's enough snow before dark, you can build a snowman. I'm going to go take care of the cattle now, so we can both stay out there with you."

"Thanks, Bruce!" She threw her arms around him and kissed him.

"How about a little more than that," he teased. She laughed and rubbed her body against his rising dick.

"I'll take good care of that when we finish playing in the snow," she said with a wink.

"Yeah, an hour out in the snow will have my balls so blue they'll never thaw out again," Bruce complained.

Kate laughed and ran back to the kitchen to fix something for dinner. She decided on a thick stew that could simmer while they were outside. She used deer meat this time and plenty of potatoes and carrots as well as a jar of her tomatoes from the garden. Once it was simmering on the stove, she hurried to look out the kitchen window. She was excited to see that it was snowing hard now, and there were at least four inches on the ground, judging from how much the porch steps were covered.

Nearly an hour later, Bruce and Marcus walked back inside, shaking off the cold and the snow on her kitchen floor. She quickly mopped it all up and fixed them some hot cider to warm them up.

"Looks like a good six inches or more out there, Kate. Should be enough for you to make a decent-size snowman." Marcus took his mug and sipped the concoction.

"Remember, you follow our directions and don't get out of our sight," Bruce said.

"I'll stay right where you put me," she promised.

They warmed up by the fire in the living room then everyone put their coats and gloves back on to go outside. Kate shoved her feet down in the boots and realized they were a little too big for her for some reason. They had been fine earlier in the season. She must have stretched them.

They filed outside, and Bruce planted her in a clear spot within sprinting distance of the back door should she need to run for it. The wind was softly blowing the snow around, but it wasn't nearly as cold as she had worried it would be. She laughed in glee and began to mound up snow to make a snowball so she could make the base for the snowman. Marcus laughed at her attempts to get it rolling, but he and Bruce were taking their job of watching out for danger seriously.

Kate finally got the ball rolling between the two men. She pushed and shoved until she had a two-foot-high base. She patted it down to make a flat area at the top to hold the next ball. By the time she had the second ball situated on top of the first one, she was out of breath and laughing so hard she hurt.

"You about finished, Kate?" Bruce asked.

"Just a minute. I need one more to make the head."

"Hurry it up, baby. It's going to be dark soon," Bruce told her.

Kate worked harder to make the head in record time. She managed to get it on the top and soon had the carrot nose, with a wart on it no less, situated in the middle of the face with potato eyes and cut potato wedges for a mouth.

"What do you think?" she asked.

They both walked over and looked at it with her. Bruce hugged her.

"Baby, you did great. It's a beaut."

"I think it looks just like him, honey," Marcus teased.

"Okay, let's go inside." Bruce had her hand, and they walked toward the house.

Marcus yelled *hurry*, but it was too late. The wolves were on them in an instant. Kate curled up in a ball and covered her head with her hands, but they dug at her coat. Then the men were there with the rifles. She heard them calling to her, but she couldn't move. She was pinned beneath the massive beasts. Pain exploded down her back and through her hands and arms. She screamed over and over, but couldn't do anything to get them off of her. Finally after what seemed like forever, a rifle report and then another sounded near her ear.

Please don't let them kill me.

She didn't want to be mauled. She couldn't imagine having a ruined face or body and living with it. Her ears were ringing from the guns, but somewhere she heard the men shouting at her again. Then hands were pulling at her trying to get her to unwind from the ball she'd made herself into.

Then someone picked her up and carried her inside and up the stairs. She felt her clothes tearing as they cut them off of her. She nearly screamed when they pulled them off her back, but instead, she passed out from the pain.

* * * *

"No, no, no," Marcus was chanting as they slowly removed the clothes they were cutting off of Kate. Her back had deep furrows where the wolves had tried to dig her clothes off of her. The cuts on her back would need stitches.

"Marcus, calm down. She's alive. We've got to keep our wits about us and get her cleaned up and sewn up as fast as we can. Once she wakes up, it will hurt her. I don't want to hurt her any more than she already is."

"Okay." Marcus swallowed.

Bruce had to keep repeating to himself that she was alive. All he could see in his head right then was the wolf's fangs at her throat. He still didn't know how bad she was because they hadn't gotten to her front. Now that she was unconscious they would be able to lay her down. They had her in the bathroom on the counter.

"Okay, let's roll her over and look to see if she's hurt around her neck or chest." Bruce helped his brother roll her over.

They stopped for a second when she moaned. Then they finished rolling her over, and Bruce nearly got sick. She was covered in blood around her face and throat. He quickly cut off her clothes and found that her chest was unharmed, as was her stomach.

"Get some hot water in the tub, Marcus. We're going to have to use towels to clean her up so we can see where she's hurt. Right now it looks like her face and neck."

"Fuck, did they tear her throat out? How is she still alive?" Marcus had tears in his eyes as he filled the bathtub up with water.

They soaked towels and began gently patting around her face until they had the blood off. She had a deep cut on her cheek and under her chin. They began cleaning her upper chest and neck only to find that she had one deep slash across her neck that would need stitches, but that was it. Bruce sighed in relief. She wasn't safe by any means. They still had to worry about infection as well as shock.

"Let's finish cleaning her up. All of the blood must have come from her back. It rolled down to her face and neck." Bruce soaked his cloth and started over cleaning her up.

It took them nearly twenty minutes to get her completely clean. By then she was moaning again. They settled her on the bed on top of several towels and began sewing her back up. She would have some serious scars, but Bruce didn't care. All he cared about was that she was alive. He hadn't failed her.

The only problem was that he now knew that he loved her. His heart had nearly broken when he saw the wolf's fangs going for her throat. He just knew she was about to die. Nothing he did would save her. But something she did had. She'd rolled up in a ball and protected her face and neck and belly. Even her hands hadn't gotten the damage he would have thought they would have.

They worked on her back then Marcus worked on her hands while Bruce sewed up the cut on her cheek and under her chin.

"Most of what is on her hands are punctures. I can't sew them up, Bruce. She'll have to let them heal on their own."

"We need a couple of bags of snow, Marcus." Bruce covered Kate up to keep her warm.

"I'll be right back." Marcus hurried out of the bedroom.

Bruce knelt on the floor by the bed and smoothed her hair out of her eyes. They had her on her side to keep off her back but still allow her to breathe easy.

"Baby, I'm so sorry. I thought we were watching. I swear we were trying to watch for you." He swallowed around the knot in his throat.

He leaned in and whispered in her ear. "I love you, Kate. I guess I always have. I didn't want to because it hurts too much to love someone then lose them. I'm sorry, Kate."

She opened her eyes and looked at him. He couldn't tell if she really saw him or not. Then she closed them again.

"Here." Marcus handed him the plastic bags of snow.

Bruce held one under her chin and one on her cheek. He wanted to keep the swelling down as much as possible. Kate moaned and tried to turn over, but Marcus held her still so that she wouldn't roll over on her torn up back.

"Baby, can you hear me?" Marcus asked. "I love you, baby. You're going to be fine. Just remember that. You're going to be fine."

"Marcus, we did the best we could do. I know we did. Was I wrong to not want her outside?"

"No, but you can't keep her sequestered inside for the rest of her life. She would grow to hate us if we didn't let her out at all."

"I know that, but I thought if she hated me and loved you, everything would work out. She didn't hate me though. She kept trying to get me to love her. She didn't know that I already did."

"She's going to be okay though, Bruce." Marcus grabbed his brother's face and stared him in the eyes. "She's going to be okay."

"If we can keep the infection away. I'm going to go fix something for her to drink. You watch her. Don't let her roll over on her back if you can help it. It will only hurt her more."

Bruce walked out of the bedroom and down the stairs to the living room. He had just turned off the stove and poured a glass of water when there was a knock at the door. Bruce sat the glass down and grabbed his gun. He looked out the door and sighed.

Opening the door, he let Joel, Jonathan, and Leigh inside.

"We heard gunshots and came to see if you needed help," Jonathan said. The men had their rifles with them.

"Wolves attacked Kate," Bruce said. He had to stop. He was choking up like he was going to cry.

"Is she okay?" Leigh asked.

"It's bad. She's alive, though." Bruce looked off to the side to try and get control again.

"I'm going upstairs to see about her," Leigh said, looking at Joel.

"Do you want us to go get Brice? He's a paramedic," Jonathan said.

"I think we've done everything we can do. If she doesn't get an infection, she should be okay." He swallowed hard.

Joel clasped him on the shoulder.

"If you could stick with Marcus in case he needs anything, I need to see about the dead wolves," Bruce finally managed to get out.

"I'll go up and see about them," Jonathan said.

"I'll help you." Joel headed for the kitchen.

Bruce followed him. He appreciated the help. He would be better able to control himself and take care of the mess with someone else around. Without the help, he would likely be a sitting duck for another wolf. All he wanted to do right then was sit down and cry. He had never cried a day in his life. Not even when he'd lost Irene.

Chapter Seventeen

Kate slowly opened her eyes to find Bruce sitting in a chair by the bed. His eyes were closed. She was on her side, and her back screamed with pain. She felt her face and found a bandage on her cheek. She started to pull it off, but Bruce stopped her.

"Easy, baby. Don't mess with that. You have a couple of stitches there."

"My back hurts," she whispered.

"I know, baby. I don't have anything to give you. We don't have any painkillers that aren't too old." He leaned forward with a glass of water. "Drink some water for me so you don't get dehydrated. I'll fix you some whiskey tea for the pain in a little bit."

"Where's Marcus?"

"He's asleep next to you over there. Only one of us is sleeping at a time right now, because we don't want to hurt you."

"What about the animals?" she tried again.

"We're taking care of them, Kate. Don't worry about anything. Concentrate on getting well."

"Why did you save me?"

"What are you talking about?" Bruce looked confused.

"I'm a freak now. I'm going to be all scarred up. You'll never want to look at me again. Marcus will hate it."

"I don't want to hear you talk like that, Kate." His voice was strained now. There was anger in it.

"You're not going to want to look at me like this," she said again with tears falling from her eyes.

"Baby, I love you. I don't care what you look like. You're my life, Kate."

She swallowed around the knot in her throat. It hurt under her chin to do it. She felt like a mess. Now, when she was a disaster, Bruce told her he loved her. How could she believe him when he never told her before?

"What is it, baby?" He smoothed away the tears from her eyes.

"Why are you telling me you love me now? You never have before."

"I was fooling myself into thinking that I shouldn't love you, so I could take better care of you. I was wrong. I loved you anyway and still didn't keep you safe. Nothing I could have done short of not let you out of the house would have prevented what happened. I'm sorry, baby. We tried to keep them off of you."

"I know. It was my fault for wanting to play like a child. I'm not a child. I'm a grown woman. I should have acted like one and this wouldn't have happened." The tears flowed harder now. She hurt all over, and it was all her own fault.

"Baby, you should be able to play and have fun. What's life if all you ever do is work? The fact is, you could have been attacked anytime we went from the house to the chickens or the barn. I don't know why they didn't attack one of those times. Then it would have only been one of us with you instead of the two of us like the other day." Bruce cupped her cheek on the opposite side of her hurt one.

"Is she awake?" Marcus sat up on the other side of the bed.

"She's awake. Easy back there, her back is hurting her," Bruce said.

Marcus eased off the opposite side of the bed and walked around to crouch by her head.

"Hey, baby. How are you feeling?"

"I'm okay. My back hurts." She noticed that, like Bruce, Marcus had cuts around his hands, but nothing like hers.

She pulled hers out of the covers and winced at how they looked. They were swollen and discolored. The wolves had bitten her hands trying to pull them away from her head. She was scared to even imagine what her back looked like. She could still remember them digging at her back through her clothes.

"Marcus, sit with her. I'm going to go make her some whiskey tea. It will help the pain some."

"I'm right here. I won't go anywhere." Marcus took Bruce's chair and leaned forward to kiss Kate gently on the mouth. "Do you need anything else?"

"No. I'm sorry, Marcus." She sniffed and couldn't control the tears that continued to flow.

"What are you sorry for? You don't have anything to be sorry for, baby."

"I shouldn't have made that snowman."

"Nonsense. We enjoyed you making that snowman. It wasn't your fault. It could have happened at any time, like Bruce said. We're damn lucky it didn't happen when we were going to and from the barn one morning. Neither one of us would have made it."

"How many were there?" she asked.

"Four of them. Three jumped you, and one jumped Bruce. I managed to shoot one of them that you kicked off before it could jump back on. By then, Bruce had killed the one on him. Then we both pulled on the last two that were on you. I shot one point blank in the head when I had a clear shot away from you. Marcus shoved the gun almost through the other one before he shot it."

"I never even felt them around us. I should have known they were there. I always knew before when there was one around." She looked down at the floor. "How bad do I look?"

"Baby, you don't look bad. You look like you hurt. "

"Don't, Marcus. Don't lie to me. How bad is the cut on my face?"

"Baby, it's just a scratch with two stitches. That's all. You'll see when we take the bandage off tomorrow. We wanted to keep it covered so we could put ice on it some to keep the swelling down."

"What about my neck? I can feel the cut there."

"It's pretty long, baby, but it will be a small scar. Don't worry about the scars now. Just concentrate on getting well. I miss holding you, baby."

"I don't want to look like a freak, Marcus. I feel like one already."

"Shhh, here comes Bruce." Marcus cupped her other cheek in his hand.

"Here's the tea, baby. Do you think you can sip it with this straw?" Bruce held the cup for her while she sucked through the straw.

She managed to get a good bit down her before she couldn't drink anymore. It burned going down. He'd evidently put a lot of whiskey in it. She could already feel herself drifting in and out of consciousness. The pain in her back dulled to an ache, and her face no longer worried her. She smiled despite the pull to her stitches. She'd made a lovely snowman until the wolves had destroyed it.

With that last thought, she fell asleep.

* * * *

The next time Kate woke up, it was dark, and she couldn't see much of anything in the dim moonlight. She looked over, and sure enough, Marcus was in the chair. That meant that it was Bruce in front of her. She was cold. She rolled farther over onto her stomach and wrapped her arm around Bruce's chest and her leg around his leg.

"What's wrong?" Bruce immediately asked.

"Bruce? What's wrong?" Marcus's voice whispered through the dark.

"She's awake. Hold on." Bruce rolled over on his back. "What is it, baby?"

"I'm cold."

"I'll cover her up on the back better."

"Please get in bed with me, Marcus. I want you with me."

"I'll get up, Marcus, and you can get in with her."

"No!" she cried out. "I want you both with me. I'm so cold. I need you."

She couldn't help the tears in her voice. Her back ached, and her head hurt. She was scared and knew it wouldn't be long before her men wouldn't want to look at her in the light of day. Right now, it was dark and she could pretend they wanted her.

"I'm scared I'll hurt you, baby." Marcus knelt by the bed and ran a hand over her hair.

"Please, Marcus. You don't have to touch me. Just be in the bed with me. I need you there."

"Bruce?" Marcus asked.

"Get in the bed, man. She's not going to calm down until you do."

He rolled over so that he was on his back and she could climb on top of him. She wrapped her arms around his chest and laid her good cheek against his chest. She felt it when Marcus climbed into the bed behind her. The dip of the mattress gave him away. She waited for him to touch her, but he didn't.

"Marcus?"

"Yeah, baby. I'm right behind you."

"Touch me somewhere. I'm so cold."

"Ah, honey." He moved behind her again.

She waited and finally felt his warmth close to her back. He began stroking her hair with one hand. She cried in earnest now. She would lose them for sure if she looked as bad as she feared she did. She could remember the tearing of her back with the wolves' claws and the bite on her cheek. She didn't remember the one on her neck, but it was minor compared to the rest.

"Easy, baby. If you're going to cry like that we're going to move. I'm scared we're hurting you." Bruce's voice rumbled in her ear pressed as it was to his chest.

"I love you, Bruce. You, too, Marcus. Please don't hate me."

"God, baby. We don't hate you."

"I can't imagine looking like this for the rest of my life."

"Kate! You listen to me," Bruce began. "Tomorrow, we'll show you what you look like. You don't look bad. You're still the same Kate from before the attack. Nothing has changed."

She didn't say anything more. She just soaked up their warmth and wished things could have been different. She remembered how it felt to be between them when they made love and how much she wanted that again. Her belly hurt. She felt sick at her stomach.

She lay still waiting on it to pass, but after a few seconds she knew she was going to be sick.

"Sick, bathroom," she managed to get out as she tried to climb over Bruce.

He was instantly up and helping her get to the bathroom. She cried from the pain to her back but soon forgot it as she heaved over the toilet. She didn't have anything really in her stomach to throw up. How long had she been unconscious?

"Easy, baby. God, baby, I know it has to hurt." Bruce was right there with her. Marcus stood at the sink wetting a cloth for her.

He handed it to Bruce, who laid it across her forehead then gently wiped her face.

"What is today?" she asked.

"Um, it's Thursday, Kate. Why?"

"I've been asleep for three days?" she asked.

"Off and on. You've been awake several times."

She thought about it and realized she was probably pregnant. She hadn't had her period in nearly six weeks now. She hadn't worried about it since she wasn't always regular, but after getting sick…

"What is it, Kate?" Bruce demanded.

"I–I need to get up." She pushed to her feet to stand up. It pulled at the stitches in her back, but she didn't care. She needed to stand up.

Bruce and Marcus both helped her stand. She leaned over the counter to take some of the pressure off the stitches. Marcus had lit a lamp for them in the bathroom. She pulled off the bandage from her face and felt the tears well up in her eyes again. She swallowed them down. She couldn't afford to cry anymore. Then her eyes went to her neck and she nearly passed out. The wolves had almost gotten her throat. She was lucky to be alive.

Ten minutes ago, that wouldn't have mattered to her. She had been so afraid that her men wouldn't be attracted her that it was all she could think about. But now she had someone else to think about. She might not look very good anymore, but she would not give up with a child on the way. She needed to lay back down now. She was exhausted.

"Going to lie down again." She turned to head toward the door.

Marcus grabbed her upper arm on one side, and Bruce took the other one. They slowly shuffled toward the bed again. She needed to tell them, but decided to wait until she could get up and move around. She didn't want to be stuck in the bed when she told them in case they didn't take it well.

She really had no idea how they felt about children. Surely they realized it was inevitable unless she was unable to have kids or both of them weren't able. She swallowed, trying to keep from getting sick again. Once she made it back to bed, she crawled in and sank to the mattress in bliss. It felt so good to lie down again.

Bruce climbed in on one side of her and Marcus on the other. They each touched her hair and anywhere they could that wouldn't hurt her. She lay there thinking about having a baby and what that meant to her. She would be busier than ever, and keeping the baby safe would be the most important thing. Maybe they could put a fence around the yard. She continued thinking long after the men fell asleep again.

When the sun rose, she was once again lying across Bruce's chest with Marcus plastered to her back. It didn't hurt. In fact it felt good to feel him tight against her. She knew the moment he woke up. He stilled and cursed.

"It's okay, Marcus. You're not hurting me. It feels good to have the pressure there."

"I'm scared to move, baby. I'm scared I'll pull on one of the stitches and hurt you."

"I'll be fine. Go ahead and move. I'm going to have to get up soon anyway and go to the bathroom."

Her cheek was itching and her neck hurt some. She must have had it in a cramped position for a while. She waited for Marcus to get up his nerve to move. She knew it would hurt, so she prepared herself so she wouldn't upset him by crying out. When he finally moved, it wasn't as bad as she had feared. She managed to grunt and lean over Bruce a little more.

"You okay, baby?" Bruce's voice reached her ear. He was whispering.

"I'm fine.

"Baby, did I hurt you?" Marcus was kneeling in front of her now.

"Guys, I'm fine. I need to get up and go to the bathroom though."

"Let me move out from under you, and you can just throw your legs off the edge of the bed and we'll help you sit up." Bruce waited for her to move off of him.

She managed to roll to her side and waited as he scooted out from under her. Then she let them move her legs to the edge of the bed and she used the palms of her hands to pull up herself up. They weren't cut up like the backs of her hands and lower arms were. Once up, she breathed awhile to wait out the dizziness then she stood up and let them help her to the bathroom.

Afterwards, she insisted on a wearing one of their superlarge T-shirts and a pair of panties. She wanted to go downstairs and sit on the couch.

"You'll get tired and need to lie back down soon, baby. The trip up the stairs will wear you out." Bruce helped her step into her underwear.

"I'll be fine. I need to get downstairs."

"Why do you need to be downstairs?" Marcus asked.

"Because you need to see about the animals and I want to be close so you don't have to climb the stairs so much to see me." She started walking toward the door to the hall and the stairs.

"Wait, baby. Let me help you." Marcus took her upper arm and walked with her. Bruce followed behind them.

It took a good two minutes to make it down the stairs because she had to stop and rest several times. The stitches pulled when she put her foot down to the next step. She hadn't counted on that.

"Damn, that nearly wore me out," Marcus said.

"It did wear me out." She smiled despite how it felt to her cheek. "I'm going to need blankets and a pillow, guys."

"I'll get them," Marcus said and hurried back up the stairs.

"I'll get you something warm to drink. Do you want some whiskey tea or whiskey cider?" he asked.

"Just some cider. No whiskey, I don't need it right now." She had no plans to drink any more of it, either. It wasn't safe for the baby.

"I'll fix you some scrambled eggs, too. You need to eat something."

"Thanks, Bruce."

Marcus came barreling down the stairs with two blankets and two pillows. "The pillows came off the other beds so you don't have to worry about them going back upstairs. We've got plenty of blankets."

"Oh, I almost forgot. When you got hurt, Joel, Jonathan, and Leigh came over. They heard the gunshots and came to see if we needed help."

"Oh my God! Did they see me like this?" Kate was appalled.

"The guys didn't. Leigh did and helped us get you comfortable. She's been sending one of the guys over almost every day to find out how you are."

"They are good people, Marcus," she said.

Bruce walked in with a plate of scrambled eggs and her cup of cider. "Who's good people?"

"Joel's family," Marcus said.

"They helped me clean up the mess out back when they came over. You're right. They are good folks." He sat the plate of eggs on her lap.

She was leaning forward to keep her back off the back of the couch. She would lie down once she finished eating. She needed to eat, though. She took a bite and had to smile when she realized it wasn't her cooking. Bruce had done the best he could. She managed to eat almost all the slightly overcooked eggs. Once she finished she sat the plate on the coffee table and finished drinking the cider. Then she stretched out on her side with her head on one pillow and her arm over the other one.

"You okay now?" Bruce looked worried.

"I'm fine. You two go do whatever you need to do. I'm going to take a nap now."

She was slowly becoming used to the idea of being pregnant, but she needed more time to think about it. She needed to be prepared for whatever the men did or said—or didn't say.

Chapter Eighteen

"Marcus. I think Kate is pregnant." Bruce finally spit it out after beating around the bush for twenty minutes while they rounded up the cattle.

"What?" Marcus nearly lost his balance on the horse. "Are you sure?"

"She's late. I sort of keep up with that so we don't push her when she's not feeling well."

"And she was sick early this morning," Marcus added. "Ah, hell."

"What do you think about it?" Bruce asked his brother.

"I'm—I'm not sure. I mean, we knew it would happen, but now, when she's hurt and when we have this wolf problem?"

"Well, before we go back in that house, we better have things settled in our heads. She's going to tell us soon, and if we're iffy on it, she's going to be upset. She doesn't need to be upset and pregnant and hurt, Marcus."

"Well how do you feel about it?"

"I'm like you. It's not the best time, but then when is the best time? We're not the only ones dealing with this now. Brandon's family and Brice's family are in the same boat." Bruce sighed and shot off to rein in one of the cows that had started off in the wrong direction, again. "I swear, that is going to be the first cow we're going to kill when we start selling meat."

Marcus snickered but quickly sobered up when Bruce frowned at him.

"Look, we just have to accept it and present a solid front that we're okay with it." Marcus sighed.

"I can do that. I'm just not sure we can pull it off. She's going to know we're hiding how we feel if we act like we're perfectly happy about it."

"I'm actually a little excited, Bruce. I'm just worried."

"Yeah, I guess so. I can remember wanting children with Irene, but it never happened. Then she was gone. I wasn't letting myself think about Kate like that because I didn't want to fall for her, so I don't know how I feel right now."

"What are we going to do when it's time for her to have the baby?" Marcus's face grew pale, and Bruce had to chuckle.

"We deliver it. That's what we do."

"Maybe we could get one of the other women to come over and help her," Marcus suggested.

"She's going to expect us to help her, Marcus. You better get that into your head now." Bruce turned the cows closer to the fence line and began driving them toward the house. They kept them close to the house at night so if they heard anything, they could come out with their rifles.

Marcus pointed toward the house. "Look. It's Joel. I bet Jonathan and Leigh are at the house wanting inside. Kate can't get up and let them in."

"I'll let them in. You finish out here," Bruce said.

Marcus nodded and moved up to run the herd closer while Bruce took off toward the house. He met Joel halfway there.

"Let me borrow your horse, and I'll help Marcus finish up the cows while the women visit."

"Thanks, Joel. I appreciate that." He climbed off the horse and handed the reigns over to the other man.

He hurried to the back door and was halfway across the kitchen when he heard Jonathan and Leigh laughing. How had they gotten in?

"Hey, Bruce. Let Leigh check Kate out real quick. She got up and let us in. We didn't realize she was downstairs and would come to the door. I'm worried about her." He ushered Bruce back into the kitchen and closed the door.

"She's fine. I wouldn't have dragged you off if I was really worried."

"They want to girl talk." Bruce finished for him.

"Yeah, that's what I figure."

"How about some coffee?" He got up and put the water on to boil in the pot.

"How is she really doing?" Jonathan asked.

"She's doing really well. She's depressed some about the scarring, though."

"I understand Heather went through that, but the baby took her mind off of it."

"Well, we seem to be in the same boat. Don't say anything, because she hasn't told us, but we're pretty sure she's pregnant."

"Congratulations!" Jonathan shook Bruce's hand until he thought it would fall off.

"Thanks, I'm not sure how this is going to work out, with everything happening right now. Between her being hurt and the wolves, I'm really worried."

"Well, we've gotten everyone involved with the idea of a communal garden. We can grow more like this than separately and keep the women safer."

"We're also talking about running one herd of cattle. One group works them for a week at a time and we rotate them around so that everyone takes a turn and no one person is overworked when we have families to take care of."

"Sounds like an interesting plan. It might work." Bruce was willing to entertain anything that would help keep his family safe. Now more than ever.

"Um, guys? Can we have some cider?" Leigh walked into the kitchen with a smile. "She's fine, Bruce. She didn't pull any stitches or anything."

"Good. I never dreamed she would try to get up and answer the door. She's just that stubborn." Bruce poured up some cider and set it on the stove to warm. "I'll bring it to you when it's warm."

"Thanks." She closed the door behind her and returned to the living room.

"So what are you going to do when she tells you?" Jonathan asked.

"I don't know yet. We don't want her to think we're mad or upset really, but if we act happy and excited, she's going to know something's up."

"Tell her the truth. Tell her you wish things were better to raise a child, but you're happy if she is. That's the bottom line, isn't it?"

"I guess you're right." He turned to the stove. "Looks like the coffee and the cider are both ready."

* * * *

The men saw Joel and his family out while Kate rested on the couch. She was exhausted from sitting up so much, but she had refused to lie down while the guys were in the room. She was very thankful for the blankets that covered her from neck to toe.

"Baby, how about we fix you something to eat and then we help you upstairs to bed. You're so exhausted, you're pale." Marcus kissed her cheek and then her forehead.

"That sounds like a good idea to me," she agreed.

Bruce disappeared into the kitchen for the next thirty minutes then emerged with a bowl of soup and some cheese. She sighed. She loved the cheese they made with the milk. It would give her the protein she needed for the baby. She grinned and ate the cheese, then worked on the soup. By the time she had finished the bowl, it was shaking in her hands.

Marcus took it from her and set it on the coffee table. She smiled at him.

"Let's get you upstairs," he said.

Bruce stood up, and between the two of them, they managed to help her up and up the first few steps. She rested every couple of steps. It frustrated her to have to stop so often. She was afraid the men would be impatient with her. Once she was on the bed, Kate sighed and closed her eyes.

"We're going to go downstairs and eat and clean up, Kate. Do you need anything before we go?" Bruce asked.

"I need to tell you something," she said.

"What, baby?" Marcus asked.

She eyed them. They looked entirely too sure of themselves. They knew. She huffed out a breath.

"I'm pregnant, but I think you already knew that." She watched them closely.

"We guessed, baby. You were sick this morning, and you're late." Bruce smiled.

"You kept up with my periods?"

"Sort of."

Hmm was all she could think of to say.

"Everything will work out fine, baby. Just relax and take care of yourself." Marcus sounded more like what she had expected from him. Worried.

"Go eat and clean up. I don't want to come back to find my kitchen a complete wreck," she fussed.

"We'll make sure it's in good shape when you get well enough to do anything in it, Kate." Bruce grinned and pulled Marcus by the arm toward the door. "Just holler if you need us for something before we get back up here."

"I'll be waiting on you. It's cold in this bed alone." She smiled, wishing the stitches didn't pull in her cheek when she did to remind her they were there.

As if knowing what she was thinking, Bruce walked over and kissed her gently on the lips.

"The stitches can come out in another three days."

"Thanks, Bruce." She touched his arm with her hand. The glaring scratches and sutures reminded her of what her back would look like. Her mood soured a little bit after that.

Once the men had headed downstairs, she stretched out to relieve some of the pressure on her back. Then she allowed herself a little pity party about the mess her back and arms were in. She could almost deal with the scratch on her cheek, but add to it the ones on her back and her arms and she was sick about it all over again.

She must have dozed at some point because when the men emerged from the shower, she started and jerked at the stitches in her back.

"Easy, baby. You'll hurt yourself," Bruce warned. "We didn't mean to scare you."

"I'll be glad when these are out of my back. I can't stand the pulling."

"I know, Kate. It won't be much longer." Marcus climbed into the bed behind her and laid his hand on her hip.

Bruce eased into the bed and lay on his back so she could drape herself over his chest and relax. Sleeping on him helped keep her warm, and she didn't try and turn so much that way. She doubted that either man slept well, but she didn't know what to do about it. She needed them close to her.

"What are you thinking about, Kate?" Bruce asked.

"Just that I love you both so much, and I'm scared for the baby. I mean, how do we keep a child safe? Children don't always mind when you tell them something."

"We'll manage, baby. Maybe put up a fence around part of the back so we don't have to worry quite so much." Bruce ran a hand through her hair.

"I like that idea," Marcus said from behind them.

"We'll have to go to one of the cities to get the fencing materials," Bruce said.

"I'll have to have maternity clothes soon anyway. That and baby things."

"We'll plan a trip as soon as you're well enough to travel, baby. We're not leaving you here, and it will take both of us to load the fencing material." Bruce's voice rumbled in her ear.

"You know, we could leave her with one of the other families that day," Marcus suggested.

"No!"

"I think that settles that," Bruce said with a soft chuckle.

"You're not leaving me behind. I need to pick out the right clothes and things. Just giving you a list won't work."

"You have to stay in the truck except when we are with you while you look," Bruce warned.

"No problem. I can read while you work on the fence stuff."

"I guess you're coming with us, then," Marcus said. "I'm going to worry the entire time we're gone."

"You would have worried about me while you were gone anyway," she fussed.

"True," Marcus agreed.

"Get some sleep, baby. You've had entirely too much excitement for one day," Bruce told her.

Kate lay awake for another twenty or thirty minutes thinking about being a momma and wondering how she was going to keep the men happy with her now battered body. She didn't want to lose them, but she also couldn't stand to see the pity, or even worse, disgust on their faces when they thought she wasn't looking. She finally wore herself out worrying and fell asleep.

Chapter Nineteen

Mike arrived the next day to see about her. He was almost inconsolable, and only Kate pretending that she wasn't in pain or upset over the scarring calmed him down. When she finally broke the news to him that she was pregnant, he was just as excited.

He stayed the entire day then went home that night promising to return the next day to help remove the stitches. Kate wasn't so sure that was a good idea. She knew she wouldn't enjoy that part, and her brother seeing her upset wouldn't help.

Finally, after several days of his coming to see her, she convinced him she was fine and that although he was always welcome, he didn't have to come over every day to keep her company. The arrival of Leigh to visit helped convince him that she was really doing fine.

It was decided that he would drive out to Sky Line with them when they went in two weeks. It would mean extra hands to load the fencing and an extra pair of eyes to watch for wolves. Secretly, Kate was relieved. She had worried about the guys trying to watch for wolves and load fencing all at the same time.

Several days before they were to head to Sky Line, Kate woke to find the guys still sleeping soundly. She grinned. Now was a good time to instigate some mischief. They hadn't made love to her since she had been hurt. No matter how much she had begged, they kept insisting she wasn't well enough. Deep down she thought it was because her wounds turned them off. She decided to find out once and for all.

She gently pulled back the covers to reveal Bruce's thermal-clad erection poking upward. She quickly slipped him free of the material and sucked him into her mouth before he could figure out what was going on.

"Fuck, Kate! What are you doing?" His hands immediately dug through her hair.

She ignored him and continued to lick and nip and suck until he was gripping her head with his hands.

"God, just like that."

"Bruce. What the fuck are you doing?" Marcus asked from behind her.

"I'm being attacked. Aw, fuck. Yeah, baby." Bruce tightened his grip on her hair.

Kate continued her assault on Bruce. She licked around the rim of the mushroom-shaped head then nipped at it before sucking his cock down her throat. He threw back his head and growled when she swallowed around him.

"Marcus, take care of her, man. She's fucking driving me insane."

Kate felt hands smooth lightly over her scarred back. She had to fight to keep from going still. She knew if she had, he would think he had hurt her and stop. When he began to follow his hands with soft kisses, she moaned around Bruce's cock. Her pussy was wet and her nipples hard with arousal. She soon had Bruce so wild with the need to come that he jerked back from her mouth and climbed out of the bed.

"Enough! Fuck, you're going to make me come before you do, Kate. That won't do." He and Marcus rolled her over to her back, carefully watching her face for any sign she was hurting.

She knew them too well. They would stop if she so much as grimaced. There was no way she was going to let them stop this time. She needed them inside of her, needed to know that they still cared about her. She didn't think she could handle it if they turned away from her again.

"Easy, baby. Let us do all the work."

"Please, Bruce. It's been so long. I need you."

Bruce licked his way from her belly down to her pussy. He placed open-mouthed kisses on her inner thighs then spread her pussy lips apart and tongued her slit.

Marcus licked around her nipples one at a time. Then he sucked one in, hallowing his cheeks as he applied suction to the pink nipple. When he let it go with a pop, Kate moaned. She looked down at his head as he took in the other one to tease and torment.

"You're so sweet, Kate. You taste like pure honey. I could make a meal off of you, baby." He lapped at her slit gathering all her juices with his tongue. Then he licked up to circle her clit.

She felt him enter her cunt with two fingers. She couldn't help but clamp down on them. It had been so long since she'd had anything to hold on to inside of her. She didn't want him to pull out. He groaned as she squeezed his fingers.

"Please, I need you inside of me, both of you, Bruce. Please."

"It's too soon, baby." Bruce began to slowly fuck her with his two fingers.

"No, no, no. I have to have you both. It's not too soon. It's been two weeks. Two long, lonely weeks, Bruce," Kate pleaded with him. She wanted both of her men inside of her at the same time.

"Bruce?" Marcus had his lips hovering above her breast while the fingers of one hand were kneading her other breast.

"Fuck, Marcus."

"Please, Bruce. I need to feel you inside of me," Kate begged him.

"Ah, hell."

Kate relaxed. He had given in. She would have her men and know once and for all how they really felt about her now.

Marcus rolled over and pulled her with him. She grinned like an idiot with heavy-lidded eyes as she climbed on top of him and settled her pussy over his dick. She had to work to take him inside of her. His dick was swollen with need, as were her pussy muscles. He grasped her hips and helped her push up and down until she was fully seated on his thick cock.

Bruce had moved behind them and now gently pressed against her back to lay her all the way down on top of Marcus. He laid soft kisses up and down her back, over each scar, and between every niche of her spine. Then he caressed her ass cheeks before spreading them and applying the cool lubricant from where they kept it in the bedside table. He pressed one finger inside of her back hole past the resistant ring. He pumped it there over and over while she pushed out.

After a few seconds, he added more lube and a second finger to the first. It pinched at first then gave way once he pressed passed the tight ring. She pushed out until it popped through. He pumped them in and out of her ass until she was pressing back into him with each one.

Bruce pulled the two fingers out and added a third finger this time. Kate moaned as he pressed forward with them until they eased past the tight ring. She groaned at the burn. He stilled and waited for her to start moving backward on them before he pumped them in and out of her back hole.

He finally pulled them free and added more lube before pressing his thick cock at her dark entrance. The pressure was more than she remembered. He pushed at her little rosette until finally, his dick popped through and he tunneled deep into her back passage.

The pressure was exquisite as it built inside of her. When he didn't move any deeper she squirmed between the two men. She tried to move on them, but couldn't get enough traction to either press forward on Marcus or move back on Bruce. Finally, they had pity on her and began to slowly fuck her with their heated cocks.

First Marcus pulled out while Bruce pushed forward, tunneling deeper into her body. Then Bruce pulled back while Marcus plunged into her cunt with his massive dick. Over and over they took turns inside her body as her orgasm climbed and soared higher and higher.

The sweet pinch of pain had turned to a fiery burn that was consuming and mind-blowing all at the same time. It drove her deeper and deeper into the ecstasy even as she flew higher toward her orgasm.

They fucked her fast and deep with Marcus hitting her cervix with every stroke. She needed something more. She pulled on her nipples, plumping her breasts then pinching the tips until, with one final plunge of a cock inside of her, she screamed out their names as her orgasm exploded over her. She clamped down on both dicks at once. She felt the burning heat of Marcus's release as he shot cum deep in her pussy.

Bruce's cock spurted cum into the recesses of her ass as she called out their names over and over until she was no longer able to breathe.

Then they were all three gasping for breath and fighting to regain their ability to see around the stars that exploded behind their eyes. Marcus pulled her tighter to him and kissed her face, eyes, and lips. Bruce kissed her back everywhere he could reach.

Finally, they pulled from her body, and Bruce disappeared into the bathroom to clean up. Kate heard the bath running and smiled. They were going to bathe her as well. Surely she had her answer.

Marcus climbed out of the bed then reached over and picked her up. He kissed her nose then smiled into her eyes.

"Love you, baby."

"I love you, Marcus."

"Time for a bath." He carried her into the bathroom where Bruce already had bubble bath in the tub for her. They helped her climb in then sit down.

"Is the water okay?" Bruce asked.

"Perfect." She leaned back and relaxed into the warm, soapy water. It felt so good to her now-cooling skin.

"We're going to take a quick shower. We'll be out to help you in a few minutes."

"I'm going to the one down the hall," Marcus said and blew her a kiss before leaving the room.

"Bruce?" she called when the other man stepped into the shower.

"Yeah, baby?"

"I love you."

"I love you, Kate. More than you can ever know."

Kate closed her eyes and remembered the feel of them both inside of her at once. The wonder of knowing that they loved her despite her scars had her fighting tears. They were by no means out of the woods emotionally. She knew they were worried about taking care of a child in the world they were now living in, but she had every faith they would work it out.

She loved them both with all her heart and all her soul. They may have received her as a gift from her brother, but they were her gift as far as she was concerned. The best gift a woman could have ever received.

THE END

WWW.MARLAMONROE.COM

ABOUT THE AUTHOR

Marla Monroe lives in the southern part of the United States. She writes sexy romance from the heart and often puts a twist of suspense in her books. She is a nurse and works in a busy hospital, but finds plenty of time to follow her two passions, reading and writing. You can find her in a bookstore or a library at any given time. Marla would love for you to visit her at her blog at themarlamonroe.blogspot.com and leave a comment, or her email is themarlamonroe@yahoo.com.

Also by Marla Monroe

For all other titles, please visit
www.bookstrand.com/marla-monroe

Siren Publishing, Inc.
www.SirenPublishing.com

Lightning Source UK Ltd.
Milton Keynes UK
UKHW02f1455020518
321990UK00005B/724/P